## SOUTH LANARKSHIRE LIBRARIES

This book is to be returned on or before
the last date stamped below or may be
renewed by telephoning the Library.

Kathleen Peyton spent her early life in the London suburbs. When she was seventeen her family moved to Manchester, where she studied at Manchester Art School. She has published over thirty novels and has won the Library Association's Carnegie Medal and the Guardian Award. Kathleen has two grown-up daughters and lives with her husband on the edge of the Essex marshes.

# NO ROSES ROUND THE DOOR

Tom and Jo have a beautiful house, fulfilling jobs and an amicable marriage, but Tom feels that his life is becoming increasingly sterile without children. Jo, a primary school head, cannot bear the prospect of sacrificing her career to years of nappies and prams. This matter provokes bitter clashes between them, and Tom finds himself drawn to the old-fashioned, vulnerable Camilla, whose one desire is to bear children. For a brief, blissful time, Tom manages to juggle his deep affection for Jo and his developing passion for Camilla — until a terrible tragedy occurs . . .

*Books by K. M. Peyton*
*Published by The House of Ulverscroft:*

LATE TO SMILE

K. M. PEYTON

# NO ROSES ROUND THE DOOR

*Complete and Unabridged*

# ULVERSCROFT
*Leicester*

First published in Great Britain in 1990


First Large Print Edition
published 2004

British Library CIP Data

Peyton, K. M.
No roses round the door.—Large print ed.—
Ulverscroft large print series: romance
1. Childlessness—Fiction
2. Adultery—Fiction
3. Love stories
4. Large type books
I. Title
823.9′14 [F]

ISBN 1–84395–191–6

C40762200X

Published by
F. A. Thorpe (Publishing)
Anstey, Leicestershire

Set by Words & Graphics Ltd.
Anstey, Leicestershire
Printed and bound in Great Britain by
T. J. International Ltd., Padstow, Cornwall

This book is printed on acid-free paper

Liz could have jumped it if she'd wished. When she looked back, she could see the ditch disappearing under builders' spoil. Martin's Hall was the solitary old building that had been spared in the new town's plans, and stood now beyond the railway, stranded in the middle of an estate of semi's.

'Martin's Hall owned all the land then. William the Conqueror gave it to one of his mates, and made him a knight, Sir Henry de Something. And the creeks and the rivers were like the roads then, they carried all the stuff, the corn and the bricks and things.'

Behind them, the orange street lights had just come on, and killed the setting sun. Their shadows ran right to the seawall and moorhens croaked in the rushes. They followed the ditch to where it passed through a sluice gate in the seawall. They ran up the bank, and the creek glittered at their feet. Looking seaward, they could have been Sir Henry de Something, for there was nothing but grass marsh and the smell of mud, of saltings, of bleached debris and bird bones, and the carcass of a barge on the far bank, beached and rotting.

'It's amazing,' Liz said, never having appreciated the fact.

'There was a quay here,' Daniel was chattering on. He scrabbled in the long cold

13

grass. 'Mrs Monk showed us — there is the tip of an old bollard showing somewhere — she knew where it was. She said it was Elizabethan. She said it was really busy here. The ships could turn round at high water. Not up that ditch though — they were poled up the ditch, and back again. They collected hay and took it to London. And corn and things. This creek was full of boats.'

The creek turned away from the new town in a dog's leg and joined the main river a mile away. Twenty miles eastward the river ran into the North Sea. When the wind was in the east, the new town was a cold place to live, for all its double glazing and polyurethane insulation. There was no sign of life now save the Brent geese grazing in the pasture, and the needle of a car's headlights far away on the road that followed the river down to the sea. Liz stood in the cold evening, hunched into her anorak, amazed at history.

'Did the Vikings come here?'

'Oh, yes. And smugglers. There was a fight on the river at the bottom there, and three excise men were killed. There used to be a ford there. You can't ford it now though — it's deeper now than it used to be. Before the first world war they were going to build a bridge — you know where that pub is now? There. It was to take a railway from the north

14

to the Thames, to take soldiers to France. But they never did it. They built parts of the railway though. Mrs Monk is going to show us that soon — she says if you know where to look you can see the old platforms. And down here, this side, there was a brick-building industry. The barges took the bricks away. That pond the other side of the sports pavilion used to be for the brick-building. They washed the clay or something. I can't remember. That's why that road is called Brickfields Road now. Mrs Monk says her grandfather used to work in the brickfields.'

Daniel was full of it.

'Mrs Monk's a local then? I didn't know that.'

'She knows everything.'

'She does indeed.'

'She used to swim in the creek here when she was a girl.'

'What, here?'

'Yes, at high water. She said they all did then.'

They didn't now. The mothers said it was dirty and dangerous, and they were always signing petitions to have a swimming bath built.

In the twilight the water was streaked with sunset. Liz could see how it would be, lying on your back in the summer looking at the blue sky and listening to the skylarks shrilling overhead. But modern parents here were uncertain of this nature on their doorstep; some parents had even talked of building a fence between the town and the creek, because the water was dangerous.

'You could swim here, why not?' Liz said, after thinking about it. 'The tide comes in and out twice in twenty-four hours. The water's salt, after all. Does Mrs Monk say it's dirty now?'

'No. She said it's lovely to swim here. As long as you can swim properly. She said never to come on your own, only with your parents. I could, couldn't I? You'd come? I'm good at swimming.'

'I wouldn't mind swimming here.'

'Can we do it then?'

'Yes, why not? When it gets warm.'

'Mrs Monk said — ' He was full of it, twittering and jumping about.

Liz thought of herself swimming here on summer afternoons listening to the skylarks. But the supermarket had her chained to the checkout. What could she do? Pete had been dead a year now, and something akin to ambition stirred like a longforgotten memory in what she had once called her mind. Mrs Monk wouldn't have gone into a decline, as she had. Perhaps when summer came and the

16

new sap flowed, she would find the energy to start rebuilding her life.

Meanwhile there was Daniel, her only reason for living, running for home down the winding path above the ditch, full of history and delight and what he was going to do, all as it should be. Good for Mrs Monk, Liz thought, warmed by her little expedition. Maybe she could find her way again, spurred by the example of the amazing Mrs Monk.

★   ★   ★

'I'll start the coffee in the Agnus Dei.'

'Great.'

Lunchtime concerts, the feeding of both body and soul in one hour flat, were a comforting mix of the sublime and the ridiculous. The subdued clatter of crockery would add a distant percussion to ill-timed pianissimos, the aroma of curry from the crypt spice an exquisite song. Tom liked churches used for sensible business: there was no better setting for an informal concert than between stout walls built to augment pulpit preachings. As the sound scampered round effigy and memorial, the brain absorbed an ambience incomparable. The music came with a patina of ancient griefs and glories, a sniff of plague and fire. Other times and other people touched the sensibilities; the spirit soared. To round it off with a cup of church coffee in the churchyard afterwards — a small garden between high walls, oasiswise amongst the swirling traffic — was a perfect start to another afternoon's work. Tom liked his groove.

He took his favourite pew for the day's choir recital — near the back, but away from the percolator, with a balanced view of the proceedings, unhindered by any of the wide stone pillars. Although he was a regular visitor, rarely missing a concert, he had never spoken to any members of the choir, or the organist, or rehearsal pianist, or even to the other regular visitors. He did not want his cerebral pleasure to become complicated by human considerations. Once spoken to, a choir member or fellow listener would have to be acknowledged again. A certain acquaintance, even friendship, was likely to develop, demanding involvement, conversation. Tom did not require this in his life. He was not alone in this, he noticed; as on a commuter train, one knew the faces but did not intrude. He knew intimately the faces of each choir member and the quality of each voice, the clothes they wore, who was friendly with whom, whether they had black coffee or white, sugar or not. He would sometimes recognise them in the street outside and they, usually, would recognise him with an uncertain half smile. There were about twenty of them, the sexes equally divided, the age range wide. A motley collection of, no doubt, office girls, computer hands, Lloyds underwriters, advertising hacks, cooks, shop assistants and what have you, their voices once in operation had a power to transcend their mundane occupations and play God for half an hour or so with the susceptibilities of those listening.

Tom sat back and let his senses wander. The church was small and had only a narrow façade on to a busy street, crowded in by later buildings, but the inside was a gem, uncramped and serene and full of Reformation memorials and monuments lettered in enviable scripts. A thin March sunlight gilded the pale urban faces of the singers and their words rang bell-like into the high, vaulted roof. Tom loved it, felt — as always — soothed and uplifted, and when it was finished drifted into the tiny churchyard beyond with his roll and coffee to sit and come gently back to reality. There were several benches but his favourite, with its back to the church wall, was unoccupied. The yard was mostly garden, the tombstones collected up to make a wall. In summer it was full of flowers, but now it was too early for all but a few daffodils and a hesitant lilac. A cold breeze nipped round the walls, and the congregation who were leaving through the yard walked out briskly, pulling up their coat collars. Few braved the benches; only one was occupied, and that by one of the choir, a soprano who possessed a sweet but not distinguished voice, a woman of about thirty-five. She was crying, quietly and apparently reluctantly, her face turned away.

If he had noticed before he sat down, Tom knew he would have found somewhere else to sit. But, having sat, he did not like to move obviously away. It was none of his business, women's tears. All the same, being a naturally curious individual, he found it hard to ignore the situation, although he busied himself intently with the interior of his church roll and the mixture of its contents. Cheese and tomato — it did not take long. He pretended an abstracted look, things on his mind to be considered in the tranquility of the church-yard. This was more successful: in fact he did actually start to work out what he was going to do when he got back to the office. A logo was required for a firm of drainpipe manufacturers; art applied to sewage, an intriguing challenge. Taste rather than vulgar-ity — his mind was travelling immediately with a hopeful swing — a terrier to the hole, a sniff in various directions, casting and pursuing . . . Tom could produce clever ideas with great ease, and the pleasure it gave him never failed. Work was a habit. He did his best work lying in a comfortable chair with his eyes closed, or in bed. People who did not know thought him a lazy bugger.

Everyone had gone. The churchyard was empty save for the girl. Tom had his idea and an accompanying surge of euphoria — the idea was worth four hundred quid and had taken him three minutes at the outside. He got up with his empty coffee cup, and knew he had to pass the girl to take the cup back inside.

His good feeling forced him to hesitate. He had everything going for him — a few words of comfort could hardly come amiss, especially in a churchyard . . . God is love and all that jazz.

'Cheer up — soon be dead!' he said with a quick smile.

As soon as the inane words had left his lips he was paralysed with horror, convinced that she was indeed crying for a dead beloved. There was something totally bereft in her expression as she turned towards him. He was so shaken by his lack of tact, he stopped to make things right, and only when he had put his foot in it a second time did he realise that she had not heard his first remark at all.

'I'll bring you a cup of coffee if you wait a minute — make you feel better.'

She shook her head, but he felt himself committed, and went on into the church where the ladies were just clearing up. They squeezed a last cup out of the percolator and he paid for it. He felt a fool now and hoped she might have disappeared while he fiddled with change, but when he went out she was still there, blowing her nose. She looked cold and watery but raised a very faint smile out of politeness. Tom's heart sank.

'Look, I don't want to pry into your troubles, but this'll warm you up, at least. Have it on me.'

'My dog died, that's all. It's nothing. It just came over me.'

Tom was so relieved it wasn't her mother or her husband that he smiled foolishly down on her. Thank God — a mere dog . . . he had said nothing out of place. She smiled again, taking the coffee.

'I couldn't help it. I'm so sorry — the music set me off.'

She seemed to pull herself together with a strong will. She was a rather craggy lady, with a sharp jawline and a splendid, aquiline nose. The nose ended in beautifully moulded nostrils and a curling, scornful upper lip. Yet her voice was meek, and sounded country. Tom was bad at accents and could not place it, but it was far from London. Her cheeks were pink and bright by nature — she wore no make-up at all — and her hair black and springy and rather wild. She had no London office veneer in her looks; her demeanour was ordinary; she was not particularly shy, nor yet come-on; she rather looked as if she hoped Tom would now disappear. But Tom, for some reason he afterwards could never fathom, stayed while she drank the coffee. Something to do with taking the cup back, like a gentleman.

'You're in the choir, aren't you?'

'Yes.'

'I come nearly every lunchtime when there's music.'

'I know,' she said.

As he, the audience, gazed at the choir so no doubt the choir, in song, gazed at the audience. Yet he was surprised at her 'I know'.

She drank the coffee quickly — it was half-cold, after all — and he politely took the cup back from her.

'Leave it on the seat,' she said. 'They come out.'

She got up to leave and, as they walked

down the path to the gate out into the street, Tom knew instinctively she was going to come the same way as himself, down past his office. He stood to let her go through the gate first. She walked with a long stride, almost mannish. Her shoes were flat and her clothes chosen for comfort: a grey tweed coat and a long red scarf which was half over, half under the bush of black hair. She did not care at all to make herself attractive, but Tom thought she was attractive, perhaps for that independent quality. Jo had attracted him like that, going her own way, ambitious and not bothered with improving herself to please the opposite sex, but Jo — unlike this dog-grieving choir member — had been, still was, naturally gorgeous. Most men looked twice at Jo, but it was obvious from the passing males that they saw nothing in the figure at his side. They walked in silence, and Tom found the silence awkward. He was going to say, 'Do you work near here?' but it was quite obvious that she did. He was going to ask her name, and thought it pushy. He did not, after all, want to know. Did he? What did she do? She sang. That was enough. She slipped away from him up a side street with a brief nod and he saw that she was crying again, not easily, but with a sort of tearing, angry grief.

A dog?

Tom, not into animals, did not understand at all.

★   ★   ★

'Very clever,' said Terry, when he took Tom's sketch back to his desk. 'I couldn't get beyond an arrangement of turds.'

'No. You wouldn't.'

Terry would have chatted her up, Tom thought. Terry could chat anyone up. He would have found out her name, address, telephone number, job, hobbies and favourite food in the few minutes it had taken to walk down the street. Terry lived with a girl called Matty in Camden Town, had a wife called Ann in Chelmsford and an illegitimate child in Woking, but had no troubles.

Tom had taken Terry on because he was hard-working, guileless, and had ambitions only in love, not in work. He did all the donkey-work without complaint. Tom was the sole creator, exploiting a quirky facility for humorous ideas for which he was in great demand, from newspapers, magazines and advertisers. He enjoyed his freelance status and had turned down lucrative offers from the head-hunters. He could have worked from home, but needed the stimulus of the city and its hoards to keep him in touch. His

25

talent was rare enough to make him highly-paid. He knew he was lucky.

Funny, he thought, staring out of his window on to a conglomeration of roofs, fire-escapes, chimneys, ventilator shafts and resting pigeons, how little one knew about the people one mixed with, saw every day. Or was he just not very perceptive? Even Jo was an enigma. She needn't be off school for any more than a month or two, after all — they could afford a child-minder without any trouble.

Three days ago Terry had said with a grin, 'Oh, have I told you — Matty's in the club! Cunning little bitch — meant it to happen, never told me she'd ditched the pill! You have to laugh, don't you?'

Tom had laughed.

It's what had set him thinking about the whole stupid business again.

★   ★   ★

Tom did not speak to the dog-grieving lady again when he went to his lunchtime concerts, the opportunity not arising. She did not come out into the garden again, but once she smiled at him when she left the platform. The concerts did not always feature the choir; quite often it was a quartet or a pianist. The

26

business did not give itself to making relationships. Both performers and audience alike made up a congregation as shifting and transient as the church itself patently was not, pointing up all manner of reflections on the nature of one's tiny contribution to the life of the universe as one sat gazing at the ancient architecture. Tom had virtually forgotten the lady by the time they met again.

He had finished work and was on his way home, but stopped outside a bank to take some cash out of the service-till. There was only one person in front of him; he waited with no more than the usual impatience, aware only of the hurrying crowd all round him, making for the tube station, the sharp nip of the spring air after the stuffy office. The girl in front of him moved off and he slipped his card in the slot. Somebody came up behind him; he did not glance up, intent on playing the computer game, wasting no time. He rarely fiddled about taking small amounts, only the round hundred, and reached up for the wad of nice fresh banknotes. As he pulled it out, the person behind him leaned forward and snatched it out of his hand. Tom, his reflexes very smart, instinctively swung round and grabbed the man's arm as he started to run, hanging on like a terrier. Even as the thought came into his brain — 'Is this wise in this day and age?' — the man, unable to twist free, turned sharply and with his free hand landed a punch in Tom's diaphragm that stopped all further thought of noble resistance. Tom dropped in his tracks, hit his head hard on a pillar-box and lay helpless amongst the hurrying feet.

He felt too ill for several minutes to be aware of what was happening, but as his collapse had been dramatic and witnessed by several people, he was given rather more support and comfort than is the lot of many recumbent bodies on city streets. His tie was loosened, a coat put under his head, a policeman sent for, an ambulance suggested.

'Oh, no, please,' he managed to gasp. 'I'm — I'm quite all right . . . in a minute . . . '

God knows where he'd land up once inside an ambulance, or what time he would get free. He could see a lot of legs and a few intent faces near his own. He felt ridiculous but, all the same, not quite able to do anything about it. It was humiliating, weird. He cared more about his present situation than the hundred pounds, which showed either how rich he was, or how stupid, he wasn't sure which.

'I say, if you like — my flat's quite near. Shall I get a taxi? You can stay until you feel well enough to go home.'

It was the choir lady, the dog mourner. She squatted down beside him, her expression earnest and concerned.

'It would be no trouble.'

'Thank you — yes, I'd be grateful — '

He would too, feeling such a fool, but too dizzy to procede on his way alone.

A taxi arrived and several helpers got him to his feet and handed him inside. He lay back on the seat, head spinning.

His deliverer got in beside him, after a direction to the driver. Tom heard her say Covent Garden.

'It's no distance,' she said. 'I live with my aunt. My name is Camilla Hastings.'

'Tom — Tom Monk.'

He felt dreadful. It was hard to be polite, and he made no more effort, hoping he wasn't going to be sick. He was aware that a rather amazing thing had happened, this woman coming to his rescue — although as they worked in the same area and no doubt left for home at much the same time each evening, it was no more than a mild coincidence.

She did not chat, but sat looking out of the window, her face flashing with the passing lights, the springing black hair splashed with red and green as they went over a crossing.

Her face in repose was without any sort of joy.

The journey was quite short. The taxi nosed through the masses of pedestrians that had taken Covent Garden to their own and came to rest in a very narrow street.

'My flat's here, above the warehouse. I hope you'll manage the stairs — I'm afraid there's no lift.'

'No, fine, I'll manage,' he lied.

He had to. The stairs were dark and smelled of cats. There was a handrail fortunately and with Camilla's arm strongly under his other elbow he contrived to get to her front door two flights up. She rang the bell, rather than fumble for her key, and the door was opened by an elderly woman.

Even in his dazed and unobserved state, Tom was surprised at the almost aggressive plainness of the flat, the harsh ceiling light, the awful swirly red and brown carpet. Because she sang in a choir, he had somehow expected a softly-lit, dusky, intellectual sort of place with books and records and a coffee table with shiny magazines. Not the *Sun* on a plastic tablecloth and nylon daffodils in a cut-glass vase. As she explained his arrival to her aunt, Camilla plumped up the cushions of a brown moquette sofa and gestured to Tom to sit down, which he did gratefully. It

30

was much better now, the feeling that one could relax at last a great comfort.

'Mugged, were you? Did you ever! The place is just full of foreigners these days! You can't move for them. Do you wonder?'

Auntie's voice was heavily Scottish. The man who had mugged him had looked very British to Tom, but he let it pass.

'I'll make you a good strong cup of tea — that'll make you feel better.'

Tom would have preferred a stiff whisky, but the old girl limped out into what was presumably the kitchen, and Camilla came back from discarding her coat.

As if she knew, she said softly, 'I'm sorry, there's no booze here. Auntie disapproves.' She gave him a conspiratorial smile. 'Tea is better for the head. Tell me what happened. I didn't see, too late on the scene. I just saw the crowd and had a look — and recognised you.'

Tom explained. He now felt highly indignant about the episode, so surmised that he was getting better.

'The sort of thing that always happens to somebody else. I've never had an experience like that before.'

Camilla, he could not help thinking, looked totally out of place in this setting. She wore a knitted jumper of an amazing mixture of beautiful colours and with her thick black hair and country pink cheeks she looked like an advertisement in one of those glossy magazines about living in the country, the sort of magazine that he had expected to find on her coffee-table. Yet she had this blank sadness about her that cancelled out any beauty she might have had. It couldn't still be the dog, surely? More likely the home surroundings, Tom thought, shifting his aching head away from the bright light.

'Do you have far to go — home?' Camilla asked.

'Forty miles. I get the train from Liverpool Street.'

'You can stay if you like. It would be no trouble. If you don't feel like travelling.'

Tom had no desire to stay, but very little desire to go to Liverpool Street and get on the train either.

As he hesitated, Camilla tactfully said, 'See how you feel in a hour or so. You can decide later.'

'I don't want to put you out. You've been very kind,' he said boringly.

He really was in no position to make polite conversation, which Camilla recognised, and after he had had the cup of tea he accepted the offer of an hour's kip on her bed.

'Shall I ring your home and tell them what's happened?' Camilla asked.

'Oh — yes — ' He had clean forgotten . . . he was generally home at the same hour and Jo might conceivably worry. He gave Camilla the number. 'My wife should be there.'

With that, he passed out for five hours.

★   ★   ★

When he came to, he had no idea where he was for several minutes. A street lamp shone strongly into the little cell-like room. There was a slight smell of gas; some people were passing in the street below, talking loudly about opera. The window was open, the air cool. Beyond the street lamp there was no view save of brick walls and blank windows, barred. It was like waking into a film set, totally unfamiliar. At home there were no lights, no sound save perhaps a distant dog barking. He could remember home all right but not why he wasn't there.

It wasn't until he lifted his head to look at his watch that he remembered. His head ached abominably. He groaned, the spirit deeply depressed and certainly not cheered by anything the eye could tell it: the dreary flock wallpaper the colour of porridge, the nineteen thirties dressing-table, too awful to count as period, the lampshade in bulbous silk with a slimy fringe hanging to conceal the fly-spotted bulb. Was this Camilla's taste? Impossible. So used to all the nice things he and Jo had surrounded themselves with and become completely accustomed to, he could see no redeeming feature in anything in the room. That it was Camilla's room did not make sense at all.

It was eleven o'clock. Still time to go home if he got his act together. He sat up, rather gingerly, and decided that he was recovered, although far from a hundred per cent. If he got home, he could take the day off tomorrow. No, he couldn't — he had appointments . . . oh, God, the thought of getting home and starting back again hardly six hours later did nothing to improve his spirits.

He got up slowly and put on his shoes. There was a light still in the living room, shining under the door. He knocked and opened it cautiously.

The bright glare from the ceiling had been replaced by the softer glow of a small table lamp and Camilla was reading, reclining on the sofa. The book was one of the short list for the Booker Prize (Tom always liked to know what people were reading, even in the train, where he eavesdropped on neighbouring novels unashamedly). This was all far more in the character he had cast for her — he did not know her, after all — and his spirits lifted considerably. The lovely colours of her voluminous jersey glowed in the small pool of light. She looked up, putting down her book.

'Feel better?'

'Yes, much, thanks. I didn't mean to stay so long. I really did sleep. I suppose I'd better make tracks. It's late.'

'You could stay the night, easily. It would be no trouble.'

'I don't want to put you out. I — '

'Honestly, no trouble. The end of this awful sofa lets down, and it makes a very comfortable bed. Auntie said I must ask you — she's gone to bed, I'm afraid. It makes sense to me, it's so late now.'

'It is rather.'

The gloomy night-life of Liverpool Street Station and the uncertain wait for the train did not appeal, to be sure. He wouldn't get home before one.

'You can easily ring your wife and tell her.'

He did not take a lot of persuading. He rang Jo. Jo was already asleep and gave her blessing to the idea without argument, yawning. She was blatantly unsuspicious and only mildly concerned about his health — more about the hundred pounds. Tom felt relieved. He was quite lively now, having slept so well, and his head was feeling much improved. His dice with death now seemed disappointingly trivial.

'Do you fancy some coffee? Or are you hungry — you must be! Shall I cook you something? Scrambled eggs? I could do with something myself, now I come to think of it.'

'That would be lovely.'

He was, in fact, ravenous. He followed Camilla into the kitchen, which was a sliver of a room, badly-designed and old-fashioned, but spotlessly clean and tidy. The effect of the cream tiles and brown formica and another of the glaring ceiling lights was again depressing to Tom.

'We always eat in there, carry things through. Do you want to set the table? The things are here.'

She fixed a meal briskly and Tom fetched and carried, setting ugly china on the uglier plastic cloth on the ugly table.

'There's no wine, I'm afraid — should you feel like it. Everything here is Auntie's — or can you guess? She doesn't go for life's little luxuries. I don't usually ask friends round, only in an emergency.'

She smiled briefly. Tom could see, in this bleak setting, the dog must have been a comfort.

'Was there really a dog?'

She looked surprised. 'Oh, yes. There was. He was run over.'

'It must be difficult, keeping a dog in the middle of London.'

'Yes. But walking the dog was my lifeline.'

She volunteered no more and Tom, on tea alone, felt too constrained to enquire further. He guessed to get away from Auntie, but why stay anyway?

'I suppose,' she said, 'you have a beautiful house in the country and a beautiful wife and beautiful children?'

She sounded neither bitter nor sarcastic, although her words were strange.

'I suppose yes to the first two. No to the third. No children.'

'Don't you want any?'

'I do. My wife doesn't.' How quickly they had arrived at this fraught subject — surely nothing he had said? Was she telepathic? Did she pick up one's inner preoccupations?

'She doesn't like children?'

'She loves children. She's a teacher. But she doesn't like babies, she doesn't like the prospect of having to put a baby before her job. Her job means a great deal to her. She's head of a primary school.'

'Well, I can understand that,' Camilla said unexpectedly.

'I can't.'

'Really? To have a worthwhile job, a demanding job, a job you like — that is wonderful.'

'Having your own child is supposed to be wonderful.'

'Parts of it, I suppose.' She did not sound convinced. She would get on well with Jo.

'I don't think men have any idea,' Camilla said vehemently, 'how, if you want to do something else, a baby is like a ball and chain. If you only want to have a baby, fine, or even a baby and a routine job, fine, but a baby and a demanding, full-time job — how can you, without something giving?'

'You employ someone.'

'Oh, you've no idea.'

Tom found himself feeling irritated.

'Women in good jobs take maternity leave to have a baby, and then never go back, because they like it so much.'

'Perhaps, for a few years. Then the child goes to school. How does the mother get back into a good job then, when she is rusty and life is just a rat race?'

Tom decided not to answer.

'What is your job?' Camilla asked.

He told her.

'If you took five years off, or eight, if you want two children, how would you get back

38

to where you were originally? You'd have lost all your accounts and your contacts, wouldn't you?'

'But teaching is a job that accommodates having children.'

'Being a headmistress isn't. It must be a job with a great deal of responsibility. To do it properly. That's the point — to do a job properly.'

'What do you do?'

'I work in a solicitor's office. It's not very interesting, but I'm not very clever. I cope with it sufficiently. It suits me.'

'Are you happy?' If leading questions were the order of the day, he might as well join in.

'No not at all.'

'Why not?'

'My job is a convenience, that's all. My boyfriend left me after ten years. My home is awful, as you can see. I see no prospect of change, unless my aunt dies, or I get the sack, both unlikely in the near future. I merely exist, at the moment.'

'Why do you live with your aunt?'

'Convenience originally. Laziness since.'

'When did your boyfriend leave you?'

'Not long ago. He should have gone sooner.'

'And if you could have what you want

— what would it be? Would you want him back again?'

'No, I wouldn't. He was no good to me. I don't want a man.'

'What then?'

'A baby. He made me have an abortion. Then he left me.'

Christ, no wonder . . . the weeping over the dog now made sense. The conversation had become the sort of naked confessional that occurred with passing strangers. The soft lamp and the scrambled egg had promised quite differently.

'And a place. My own place, a cottage somewhere.'

'Domesticity.'

'Yes. Boring, boring domesticity.' She smiled. 'Bliss.'

'Have you no family, except your aunt? No parents?'

'Yes. In Scotland. But there's nothing there. No work, no place for me. I don't fit in with them.'

She took his empty plate and put it with her own and took them into the kitchen. She came back with a cake and some chocolate biscuits.

'What about your parents?' she asked. 'What does your father do?'

'I don't know my father. I don't know what

he did. My mother keeps house for some horsey lord in Wiltshire.'

She looked thoroughly interested by this answer, instead of tactfully not following through the implication that he was illegitimate.

'You must have asked her, surely? Your mother, I mean. You can't not want to know about him!'

'Why can't I? He was French and she loved him. Not married, no. Just a bit before their time, that's all. He came over for holidays.'

'Why didn't he take her back? He was married, I suppose?'

'She never said so.'

She had said very little, after all. An unloving woman, on the whole, Tom had never supposed she had not loved this father of his passionately. She no longer knew where he was, she said. He had been cultured and sincere. It had finished long ago, through no fault of his. Nor of hers either. Of circumstance. She had never wished to marry anyone else. This information had satisfied Tom, but seemed to infuriate other people by its inadequacy. Was he not sufficiently curious? He must be like his father, Jo always said, as he was nothing like his mother in looks; his mother was — had been — blonde and fine-boned in the English country style, was now wiry and hard and grey, fit as a whippet, the rose-bloom cheeks weather-beaten and flicked with red veins, the fine hands roughened with work. She never left the stately home she worked in, tied by the old, decrepit owner and by the mares and foals. Tom went down dutifully at about six-monthly intervals, generally on the way to or on the way back from a walking weekend in Wales, which he liked to do alone. Jo was not a great walker. When she came he had to temper his mileage and his route; it was then a mere tripper's weekend, perfectly enjoyable, but not the burn-up his physical self enjoyed so much — between twenty and thirty miles of really hard going, up high and off the beaten track. He loved the hills passionately. Perhaps he got that from his father?

'Where do you come from in Scotland?' he asked Camilla, thinking of the places he knew, the hills he had roamed over.

'The Spey valley.'

'That's fine walking country! I've been in the Cairngorms several times. I love it up there.'

'To live? What on? Tourism?'

Her voice was scornful.

'My father runs a garage,' she said. 'Filling tourist cars with petrol. He wanted me to work on the pumps and do the books. He was angry when I left home.'

The bleakness came back into her face. She was a prickly, uneasy person, Tom decided, with little charm. But interesting. She made no attempt to attract him sexually, just as she had made no attempt to impress her personality on her aunt's awful flat. She seemed to regard life as a sort of steamroller in whose path she stood no chance.

'Have you had enough?' she asked. 'Do you want more tea?'

'No, thanks. That was fine. I mustn't keep you up.' He glanced at his watch. It was gone midnight, and Camilla was suppressing a yawn, although he felt far from tired after his deep sleep.

'I'll find you a sleeping bag. The sofa's quite comfortable. And something to read, if you like.'

'I'll try the novel you were reading, if I may.'

'It won't keep you awake, I'm afraid. It's too clever for me.'

She did herself down by habit. Tom helped her clear away and wash up and she fetched him the sleeping bag and showed him the bathroom.

'I get up at a quarter to eight,' she said. 'Now I've no dog. It used to be a quarter to

43

seven. We went out together. That all right by you?'

'Fine. Thanks for all you've done.'

'It's nothing.'

She left him and he settled down on the sofa with his good book, but his mind kept straying to the prickly Camilla, wondering what made a woman like that, the genes or the experiences?

★  ★  ★

Without Tom, Jo could not get back to sleep again after he had rung. She had not been very sympathetic on the phone — what had he said? Mugged and lost a hundred pounds? On the phone she had instinctively opted to mourn the hundred pounds but now, under the blankets, in retrospect, she was horrified at how close Tom had come to danger — and how little concerned she must have seemed to him about that. It was only just sinking in. Her Tom, cool and collected and always together, to be laid out on a London pavement by a thug! What if he had been killed?

She lay, cold without Tom, staring at the moonlit sky out of the window, planning her widowhood.

Alone, she could do exactly as she liked.

Stay at school all night if she liked, go to all the conferences and meetings she wanted to, not bother about boring shopping and meal-planning, the clock. She could have the house how she wanted it — untidy and more full of things and coloured rugs and old basket chairs that Tom said were ill-designed and only fit for a summer-house. There would be less Mozart and more McCartney; she could hog the television and not watch what Tom wanted, which meant she rarely watched at all. Not as much as Tom. She could keep cats. She needn't go to Wales or Scotland to walk on rainy mountains and stay in damp hotels, but could go on a package tour to Greece or to a hot beach in Spain. She could wear those trousers that she loved and which Tom said made her look like Charlie Chaplin.

She would be rid of her guilt conscience about not having a baby.

Oh, the heaven of it, not to carry around that load of guilt, growing heavier day by day!

She would feel ten years younger at a stroke.

The prospect of going through all that biological tedium depressed her utterly, and her horizon was filled with it like the East Anglian sky with crowding clouds, bigger and bigger every day, blotting out the sun. Every time she made love with Tom the pleasure was obscured by the guilt, as she knew the pleasure now for him was denied because of the farce it had become in his eyes. She knew she should get on with it, like taking a bad medicine, get it over. But then he would want a second one; only children should have a brother or a sister. Even she agreed with that. It would take years of precious, active, lovely life, which she could not bear to give up, not a minute of it.

There must be something wrong with her, that she could concern herself so deeply with other people's children and yet not want her own. Even she could see that it was very strange. She loved children, they were her life. But not her possession; her schoolchildren left her soul untouched. They left her whole and undiminished, they did not eat her up, they did not tangle her heart and soul and devour her time and obliterate her independence.

The baby in its pram, its cute little face and pretty ways, laid a stranglehold upon a woman. All her friends, even sensible Ros, her deputy at school, said she would succumb happily once it happened, she would never look back, she would not believe that she had ever felt as she did now. She did not believe them. The thought of babies had come to make her feel ill: the smell of babies, the

46

milky hiccupping drool of a newborn baby disgusted her; the cry of it in the night would be like a blow, the insistence of it would paralyse her mind. If she had it all wrong, she did not want to run the risk of finding out. She did not want a baby. She did not want it in her body, growing and kicking, and she did not want it in her mind over the years, threatening her tranquility. Perhaps she was sick. Perhaps she should consult a psychologist. Perhaps Tom would leave her.

This way of thinking was now becoming persistent, as Tom's pressure was becoming more insistent. The only way to resolve it would be for her to give in. It had to be resolved, for it was becoming unbearable for both of them. But why, between them, was it she that had to give way? If she held out always, as she had done up to now, would Tom accept it in time, or would he leave her for someone else?

After ten years, loving Tom had become a habit. They had a way of thinking (babies apart) in common; they were never bored with each other's company. He was kind and she respected him for his honesty and intelligence. She would never find another like Tom. She had been lucky. She had always been lucky.

She lay looking at the night sky out of the

window, thinking of being alone always, cold in bed, no one to talk to, listening to the owls.

* * *

When Tom got home the following day he told Jo what had happened in detail. The only thing he left out in his description of Camilla was her stated wish to embrace domesticity, complete with baby, rather than go on earning her living by working for a solicitor. It touched on too raw a nerve.

'Shall we go for a walk before we eat?'

He had an urge to cleanse the city's sour behaviour from his system. The air was mild and springlike and he could smell the saltmarsh and the sea.

'Down by the river?'

Jo agreed, although not with any great enthusiasm.

'I've been taking classes down there, trying to make them use their imaginations — what it used to be like. They're pretty dumb about life before concrete roads and sodium street lights.'

They drove down and parked the car by the builders' spoil heap, taking the path alongside the ditch towards the creek. When Jo had been a child, before the new town, she had gathered wild flowers on this path, and

48

won a competition at the village fête with thirty-five species. She remembered this now, with a sigh. The flowers had all gone now, save the odd hardy yarrow and a knapweed or two. There had been orchids in an abandoned garden up the hill, and shy water-rails in the old brickfields pond. That was why she used the creek to teach history, rather than nature study. New towns rather did for nature.

Not for Tom the token walk along the creekside — no, it was over the stile and out beyond the well-trodden track and the dogdirt towards the sea fifteen miles away. The seawall quite quickly reverted to bush, and the wild spinach still grew, Jo noted with satisfaction, and there was nothing before them but the wide river meeting the creek and the deserted fields meeting the sky. When they had gone far enough for Tom — too far for Jo — they sat out of the wind below the wall and looked at the river and the evening sky.

Tom remembered waking last night to the strange street light and the smell of gas and the awful wallpaper. Sometimes he thought he would like to get out of London altogether, work somewhere nearer the hills and fells; he found it hard to keep away from them for long. The marshes were good, but not like fell-walking. But this was pie in the

49

sky with Jo and her school.

'What d'you teach them then — about all this?'

'That it was the equivalent of a motorway once, full of traffic. It amazes them.'

The ribs of an old smack lay below them on the mud, like a herringbone, eaten away by the tides, only its keel held fast.

'What could that say?' Jo gestured to the ghost of times past. 'When she was new boys like mine worked on them, instead of coming to school. Now some parents won't even let them go down the creek to play. They say it's dangerous.'

'Christ,' said Tom.

'I've wondered . . . they ought to know what it's like . . . I wondered whether I could arrange a barge trip, take them for a couple of nights' sleep aboard. Nick's going to charter his barge this summer. Just an idea.'

'It would be a lot of work for you.'

'Yes. But the sort I'd like.'

'A barge'll only sleep twelve.'

'Yes, you can't get round Board of Trade regulations. It'd sleep the whole school really, but that's your safety again. Red tape. I could take twelve and if it was really popular I could do it again. Just think what an eye-opener it would be to some of them, to sail on one of those things, to sleep at night anchored offshore somewhere! I'd love to see them!'

'Who'd go with them? You, I take it?'

'Yes. It would have to be me. Can you imagine Grott?' She laughed derisively. 'Ros wouldn't be able to, although she'd love it.'

She sat chewing a stalk of grass, staring at the flooding tide coming back to the smack's ribs, pushing a scum of tidal debris on its lip.

'We did it, when I was at school. Ian took us. It was wonderful. We went ashore and explored and collected things — seaweed and stones and fishbones — we made great sheets of drawings and paintings, and we cooked our dinner on the beach with driftwood and Mr Hobbs played his trumpet.'

She laughed at the memory.

The school she worked at now, Rushden Primary, had been built on the site of the old village school which she had attended as a child. Now Rushden was one of five primary schools in the new town, but then one had been sufficient. There had been sixty pupils and three teachers: one mad, one beyond retiring age and one unqualified. They had given their privileged children an education unrivalled up to the age of eleven. The elderly crone instilled the three Rs as in dame school days, the mad headmaster with his trumpet, trombone and old-fashioned RAF moustache opened up worlds of excitement the village children knew little of, and dear Ian and his dog Bones living in a caravan in the playground was just one of them, giving his quiet life to their schemes and troubles and ambitions. The authorities in their wisdom had insisted on qualification and Ian had disappeared, no one knew where. He had been an instinctive teacher, rare and irreplaceable. They, the pupils, and their parents had accepted the education they received as normal, run-of-the-mill stuff, but it was only with hindsight that Jo understood what magic had flowed from those three ill-assorted teachers. She still remembered clearly and with joy the mad headmaster's stories of abandoning an ailing bomber by parachute and landing in the sea off the Outer Hebrides — could this have been true? — was it education indeed? Yes, to her it was a vision she needed, brought up secure and tight and safe . . . falling through the night sky into eternity, to survive and play the trombone. It was magical stuff for a child. She tried always to keep her own experience as a goal. To measure up she must supply the magic too.

'When do you plan to do this?'

'If I do — I'll have to see Nick about it. Get the governors to approve . . . it'll have to be in the holidays, I think, if it's only for twelve of them. I don't want to leave our

Crispin in charge if I can help it.'

'Won't he be applying for any headmaster-ships this year?'

'He wants mine. He doesn't want to move. His wife's on the Parish council and thinks she's the Prime Minister.'

Another of Jo's very good reasons for not wanting to have a baby. She didn't remind him of this but Tom knew. Crispin Grott was the only male teacher in her school, an ambitious young man whom Jo disliked. He was self-important, lacked humour, could not bear to be found fault with and was stiff and pompous with the children. They called him Grotty (of course). He wanted them to call him Crispin, but Jo did not allow the use of Christian names for the teachers.

'The only way I'll ever get rid of him is if he indecently assaults one of the children, which God forbid.'

'In the City, if you don't please the boss you get the sack pretty sharpish. The boss gets the sack too if he doesn't produce the goods. Why does it have to be different in education?'

Jo grinned. 'I don't make the rules. I'm open to competition.'

She was utterly confident, as always. The idea of taking a party of children on a sailing barge had taken her fancy, he could see. She

53

had sailed as a child with her father and was familiar with sailing ways and with the local coast: she would pass on her own enthusiasm to the urban-minded children in her care. She was marvellous. If he had a child, he would want it taught by someone like Jo.

He lay back on the cold evening grass and stared at the sky. The smell was elemental, of bared mud and the salt water flooding over it in its timeless tidal dance. The sky was washed-out, lethargic, waiting for dusk. An aeroplane was coming in from the North Sea, so high that it was noiseless, but given away by the vapour trails from its engines. Tom watched it idly. There was something in him lately that felt restless — as if not having his child was making him impatient instead for change of another sort, of place perhaps, or woman. An animal instinct, undesired, not at all a sensible, intellectual consideration. Perhaps he just needed a holiday.

They walked back, heading for the sunset and the sodium lights that bathed the West in a colluding glow. When they came to the top of the creek they met Daniel Weston and his mother, sitting on the wall as they had been sitting earlier, watching the encroaching tide. Daniel got up politely when he recognised his headmistress, and Liz scrambled up after him, embarrassed.

'Oh, Mrs Monk!'

'Hullo.'

Jo would have preferred to walk on, but Liz's expectant face held her back. So she introduced Tom and made some fatuous remark about the weather and Liz said, 'Daniel brought me down here, because of your lesson. I'd never come here before, I don't know why.'

'Lots of people never come,' Jo said. 'There were more people down here once, on a summer evening, when the place was just a tiny village, than now when it's a hundred times as big.'

'It's funny, isn't it? People watch the telly.'

Tom looked at Daniel and saw his slight resentment at being disturbed — just as he himself hated to meet other people when he thought himself alone. He would go out of his way sometimes, on a mountain, to avoid another person. Daniel turned his back and started skimming some stones off the path across the surface of the water. Tom, watching him, realised that he was seeing him as a son, slight and solemn and vulnerable, exactly the sort of boy he would like. He had a grave, sweet face under floppy fair hair, and a way of regarding his mother as if he was in charge, worried for her.

As Jo moved on to continue their way,

Daniel turned and said to her, 'It is all right to swim here, isn't it? In the summer. You said so?'

'Yes, quite all right.'

'Mr Grott says it's dangerous.'

'Did he say why it's dangerous?'

'The current, he said, and the mud, and the germs.'

'I don't think he knows it very well, Daniel. If it was the main river, he'd be right about the current, but it's of no consequence here at the top of the creek. The mud is dangerous if the tide's out. You can get stuck in it. But of course you only swim when the tide is fairly high, and you scarcely have to touch the mud. As for the germs — well, it's a matter of opinion. I think myself that there are probably fewer bugs to do you harm here than in a crowded swimming bath.'

'We thought it would be lovely to swim here in the summer,' Liz said.

'Well, I often do. You must never come alone, Daniel, though. You know that? You get out of your depth easily here.'

'Oh, he wouldn't do that, Mrs Monk. We'll come together. He's a good swimmer too, and very keen on it. There being no bath yet in the town, you see, he was afraid he wasn't going to get any swimming. He was a bit put off by Mr Grott saying that.'

'Mr Grott doesn't know it very well, I think.'

They continued on their way and, once out of earshot, Jo said, 'Bloody Grott. It's dangerous getting born, for God's sake.'

'Crossing the road. Driving a car. Riding a bike.'

'Using the service-till.'

'My God, yes!'

'His idea of an exciting afternoon is washing the car.'

'My mother used to ride in point-to-points. That's pretty dicey.'

'I can just see her!'

They drove home and had an amiable meal out of the freezer, and opened a bottle of wine. Jo was very taken with the idea of hiring a Thames barge for a party of her children.

'We could go and see Nick about it. We could have a trial run, perhaps. He's been working all the winter on *Adeline* and she must be almost ready to sail.'

'I wouldn't mind a weekend's sailing.'

'Good. I'll see if he can give us a date.'

'If we do . . . ' Tom reached over for the wine bottle, to refill his glass, 'it might be an idea to invite Camilla — the girl who took me home and gave me a bed last night. She was very kind. I owe her something. That might be just the thing.'

'Fine. There'll be masses of room.'

'She's a country sort of girl. I don't know how she sticks life, never getting out of the centre of London.'

'I'll fix it with Nick then, and you invite her.'

'Okay.'

For some reason, Tom felt he had manoeuvred Jo into accepting. He tried to pretend that he truly was asking Camilla to repay her for what she had done for him, but he knew there was more to it than that. What it was he carefully did not allow himself to consider.

★   ★   ★

Camilla walked home through the market and, on impulse, stopped to buy a cup of coffee within earshot of a fairly decent saxophonist busker — more to put off getting back into the flat than for pleasure. The evenings were drawing out and it was still light; if she had still got darling Danny waiting at home she would have hurried to fetch him, and taken him out to Green Park or somewhere, thrown sticks and laughed — yes laughed . . . he had had that effect, with his funny cocky expression, his ugly-sweet mongrel body poised for action, all eagerness and love. She had lavished her affection upon him in the manner of unstable single women; she had watched herself with a steely unsympathetic eye, making a fool of herself, and not heeded: Danny the uncomplicated friend, faithful to death. Animals were rocks compared with human beings. Losing Danny had been far worse than losing Jake. It was the waste of her years with Jake that she mourned, not the man. Jake had used her, but Danny had loved her, even as the light of life had faded from his eyes. How pathetic she was, that she could still cry for Danny! Despising herself had become a sour habit. She watched herself as from outside, seeing the drag that other people saw. It was up to herself now to pull herself together, make a new life as they said, but the will was hard to find. Change jobs, leave London, buy a flat, join a keep-fit class . . . oh, God, the effort! Tomorrow, tomorrow. And she saw herself again, like wet knitting abandoned.

She carried her cup of coffee to a purple-painted table, pushing away the dirty crockery. Even the once-glamorous market had become tawdry and debased, it seemed, a shifting pitch for shoving tourists and the crude young amongst whom she counted herself no longer. It had been wonderful when it was newly released from its fruit and vegetable context and the office-block plans had been miraculously defeated, all set to be the real centre for Londoners like herself, full of imaginative workshops and happenings, a place to belong to, connect with, an island amongst big business. To have an address there — how it impressed people! But somehow it was no longer attractive to her; she could not relate to the people that swarmed under the high, elegant market-hall roof, not even to much of the trendy stuff laid out for sale; she was no longer amused by the people whose job was amusing, nor uplifted by the atmosphere. Even the coffee was mediocre and the floor covered with litter and cigarette butts.

It was called depression, she supposed.

Doctors had a cure: Valium or Librium or perhaps more advanced pills that she had not heard of. Chuckle pills, as once a friend had called them. Danny had worked better, but he was addictive too. Danny . . . only a dog.

She had only herself to blame. Life was what you made it — all the clichés came readily to hand. The first thing she ought to do was leave London, where she had many acquaintances but no one she would be unhappy to leave. Even the lovely Mr Monk, like a dream, was happily married. Well, she had guessed that, but it had hurt when he had admitted it — a beautiful wife and a beautiful house in the country. Out of her masochistic habit she had almost willed him to be so endowed. His aloof air and quiet manner, his gentleness combined with a very cool and steely self-possession made him most attractive to her; she was not for fun and larks and sexuality. His style was tailormade for her depression. That wary eye and cautious appraisal was to her taste, as was the fine-drawn face, the dreamy grey eyes and slightly sad air. Other-worldly, and she would have fancied another world at the moment. Whatever had he thought? She had seen his quick horror when the flat door opened on to that stark, ugly room, and had warmed to his taste; she too had not yet learned to be unaffected by the hideous entry and dreaded it daily. Hence the procrastinating coffee, and walking Danny, before the hurrying taxi hit him.

She must leave her aunt in order to survive, however cruelly it would affect the old lady. Camilla pushed her coffee cup away and got up to leave, threading her way with difficulty through the crowded tables. The sudden movement made her feel she had come to a decision, but she knew it was all a farce, as it always had been — her intentions to improve her lot. She would look for a flat of her own, read her aunt an ultimatum ... she had made the same decision several times before, and even received a steady stream of flat descriptions from various house-agents, which she read without appetite, only noticed that the prices were rising week by week. A few more weeks and even a one-roomed pied-à-terre would be out of her reach.

But when she got home there was a letter from Tom Monk, inviting her down for a weekend, to go sailing on a Thames barge.

★   ★   ★

That evening, later, she walked down to St Katharine's dock to look at a Thames barge, to see what she was in for, and stood for a long time by the water, her hands thrust into the deep pockets of her grey tweed coat. The tide was high and the quay lights splashed orange strokes, Monet-wise, down the water where it heaved uneasily to the opening of the lock gates. There were foreign yachts with cosy cabins glowing in the dusk, the shouting of young German voices, and laughing, and a strong smell of nature — mud and seaweed and decaying vegetation. Some gulls wheeled with pale wings against a luminous sky scattered with soft stars, nothing dramatic but, for once, promising. She smiled and when she turned to walk home she forgot — for the first time — to look for Danny.

# 2

Jo tried to avoid confrontations with Crispin. The fact that he irritated her as much as he did was an irritation in itself. Jo thought she should be able to rise above it, be amused, or philosophical at least. But anything that reacted adversely upon her children Jo found hard to bear, and Crispin came into this category. Few headteachers could boast an ideal, hand-picked staff and Jo knew she was pretty lucky with hers; it was inevitable that there had to be a Crispin to redress the balance. When he had presented himself for interview, he had seemed affable enough, and the governors had been very anxious to have a man on the staff, so she had gone along with their preference. But the governors did not have to work with him.

He came to her office with a petulant complaint.

'I don't think Stevie should be allowed in the staff-room. He's no place there. He's not staff.'

'Not officially, no. But he likes his cup of tea. Where else should he go? Does he disturb you?'

'It's not that. I don't think he should be here at all.'

'Ros finds him very helpful. What is your objection?'

As if she didn't know . . . Stevie was a sixteen-year-old punk with a Mohican haircut dyed bright red, a black leather jacket and skin-tight jeans. Naturally Crispin disapproved. The jobless Stevie had come originally with his five-year-old sister when she had started school, because she had a speech defect and was paranoically shy. The mother went out to work and had been worried about the child's first few days. Jo had agreed to let Stevie accompany her, but since then Stevie seemed to have become part of the furniture. He got fed but not paid, and was now a fixture in the infants, a natural with infant minds, as attuned to the small children as Crispin, unfortunately, was not.

'He serves no purpose now his sister has integrated successfully.'

'Ros seems to think he does. She says she dreads the day when he departs. You know she calls him Stevie Wonder?'

'He has no conversation at all, and no manners either.'

'He doesn't say please and thank you, granted, but if it weren't for how he looked, surely we'd hardly notice he's here?'

'But when he's in the staff-room, he can overhear a good deal of conversation that should be confidential.'

Jo could not help laughing. 'It's not MI5! He only comes in at break for tea. Surely you can abstain from confidentialities while Stevie drinks his tea?'

She knew she should take Crispin seriously, as he took himself, but he was too preposterous. Stevie, who scarcely spoke out of the infants' classroom, had a natural empathy with small children. He did not consciously try to please them, but they all loved him. He sat all day at the back of the class on an infants chair with spindly denimed legs angularly bent and red crest nodding, like some migrating crane resting in passage, and Ros gave him the muddled children to sort out, the sad ones or the aggressive ones, and they sat on his lap and stroked his red crest and he mumbled to them, or read books with them, or drew pictures of bulldozers, and all was peace and content around him. Ros said, 'If we all had his gift, schools would be happier places.' Ros, to Jo's mind, was a brilliant teacher; she acknowledged Stevie's talent. Crispin was not only a bad teacher but too thick to acknowledge a gift in others.

'I'm sorry, Crispin, but I think we need all

the help we can get. I have spoken to him about whether he shouldn't be out looking for a job but he assures me it's of no consequence, and apparently his parents feel the same, so you can say we're keeping him off the streets. That can't be a bad thing, surely?'

Crispin put on his injured face and said, 'I just can't see that he has a place in the school, that's all.'

'The thing will solve itself. He will get tired of it soon enough, I'm sure. When the fine weather comes, probably.'

Crispin had a bland, rubbery face and sandy reddish hair that was already beginning to recede. He liked order and precision and tidiness and submission, and was a good teacher in that he cared obsessively that his children got their basic literacy and numeracy right; he was prepared to spend a good deal of overtime with his dullards. Jo had to remind herself often that he was good value on that account. But it did not make up for his lack of imagination, humour, sense of adventure, sympathy and general appeal. The children were not fond of him, as they were of Ros and Eileen and old Gwen Mason — every bit as keen on getting things right as Crispin — and the two new girls, Ann and Penny.

Worrying away at his bones, Crispin brought up another grievance before making to depart.

'Ros was saying you are thinking of taking some of the children on a sailing trip. She said it would be my form. Is that right?'

'I'm looking into it, yes.'

'I trust you won't require me to come?'

'I wouldn't dream of asking you, Crispin. I shall take them myself.'

'You will be discussing this with the governors, I presume?'

'Of course.'

Jo thought Crispin was beginning to trespass upon her authority, and said sharply, 'I believe you told Daniel Weston that it was dangerous to swim in the creek. Is this correct?'

'Yes. He asked me and I gave him my opinion.'

'Then you should get your facts right before you give opinions. There is no current to speak of at the top of creek, and the risk of danger from germs is negligible. Ask Dr Frost. Both he and I have swum in that creek for twenty-five years and come to no harm. As long as the child is accompanied and competent there is no danger. It was quite wrong of you to discourage him, Crispin. Swimming is to be encouraged, surely?'

'I'm afraid I beg to differ, Mrs Monk. In a proper swimming bath, yes, I agree, but not in that dirty creek.'

'All the same, it is safe and not to be discouraged. You understand me?'

It would have been hard, from the tone of her voice, to mistake her meaning. Crispin departed without replying, his face pouting with indignation. He had really asked for a dressing-down, Jo reckoned, but she found it hard to be amused by the incident. Crispin was so depressingly wet, the children deserved better. He was old before his time, a man who had gone for primary teaching because it was back to the womb and a chance of attaining some authority, the motivation of a weak character. He was bogged down in trivia.

Despising Crispin, Jo was clearly aware that her own curriculum vitae was not exactly an inspiration: had she any right to criticise Crispin's safety-first attitude to life when she herself had actually come full circle to teach in the school she was herself taught in? Not much sense of adventure there. What had been her own motivation for primary school teaching, if she was so quick to despise Crispin's? She had never wanted to do anything else; there had been no decision to take when she left school, it had been taken years before. Jo felt that she had a vocation. Was that arrogant? But her childhood, her student days and her teaching had all been spent virtually in the same place, a pretty damning indictment for someone criticising another for his lack of adventure.

'The trouble with you is that you are totally lacking in a sense of discontent,' Ros said to her later. 'You have always liked where you live, liked what you've got. You never want to go away because you like what you are doing here, and when you do go away you always come back saying you wished you went away more often, because it's so enjoyable. To be so happy is very tedious, you know.'

'I always thought you were one of the happiest people I know.'

'Yes, I'm happy, but I'm always wanting, aren't I? You know I hate this place — I want to go back to Norfolk but I can't because of Dave having to work in London. I would like my own school like you, but I can't because of the children — I wouldn't be able to cope.'

Ros Taylor had three children of her own, aged fourteen, ten and eight, and a class of twenty-two five-year-olds, most of whose individual mothers sent them off to school each morning with a great sense of relief. She coped magnificently, although not without the wear and tear showing at times.

'Don't you think our Crispin is happy?'

'With that wife?' Ros laughed. 'How can he be?'

'Is she that bad?'

Ros lived near the Grotts, her untidy garden backing on to the neat plot of Crispin's semi.

'Lorna's very ambitious, that's her trouble. It's she that wants Cris to get on, be a head. She's always at him.'

'I don't think he could cope with being a head. Not yet, at least.'

'He would be a very bad one. If she left him alone, he might relax and be a better teacher.'

'Poor boy. What does she do for a living? I know she commutes — probably earns more than he does.'

'And never lets him forget it, I imagine. She's something bossy in Selfridges, not sure what. And she loves being on the local council, does an awful lot of talking, I'm told.'

'I think she must have been behind getting that woman elected as a parent governor — Ann Forrester. Of all the governors, I find Ann Forrester a pain, the only one. She's not there to help and be constructive, but to criticise and find fault. Some of them are pretty ineffective admitted, but at least you know they're on your side, but with Ann Forrester, I sometimes wonder if she wouldn't be better employed standing for parliament.'

'She stood for the council but didn't get elected. Yes, she is a friend of the Grotts. I daresay they did engineer her being a governor. Get a finger in the pie.'

This conversation took place in Jo's office, the 'confidentialities' being bandied about not overheard by anyone else. Perhaps poor old Crispin did have a point . . . perhaps she had been hard on him. He could well see her friendship with Ros as favouritism, although in truth they were so similar in outlook and temperament that the deep friendship was inevitable, and would endure without work having anything to do with it. Their husbands got on too, a bonus, although sparky Dave Taylor was quite unlike Tom.

Perhaps it would be a good idea to invite the Taylor family on the Thames barge weekend . . . ? Jo was not too happy at the thought of spending the weekend with Camilla alone, as she sounded from what Tom said a rather gloomy character. The Taylor family would flesh out the party very well — or would Crispin see the invitation as favouritism? She could ask the Grotts too!

'For God's sake!' Tom groaned. 'If you ask

the Grotts, count me out.'

'It was only an idea. I thought they would be bound to refuse.'

'Don't risk it. Ros would hate it, for a start.'

'Okay. It was only to prove a point — forget it. I'll fix a date with Ros and ask Nick. And your Camilla's accepted?'

'Yes. I spoke to her at lunchtime.'

'Fine. I'll make the arrangements then.'

★   ★   ★

Camilla had almost forgotten what it was like to leave London on a Friday night and head for a weekend party. Once, it seemed, long long ago, she had indulged in such frivolities, but since getting hung up with Jake weekends had been spent cleaning his flat and ironing his shirts, eating take-away and going to a late-night movie. How could anyone have been such a fool? She could not bring herself to think about it now, it grieved her so much — her lost youth. She had been so lonely in London . . . meeting Jake, she had latched on to the routine that suited him so well. Ten years! She hadn't got herself together at all since they had parted, and was nervous of supposing that her life was now starting anew, although all her instincts were telling her that it was.

She had spent the whole week trying to decide what to wear, pretending she just wanted to be warm and comfortable. She had gone to C & A and got herself an anorak and matching trousers in emerald green which went well with the Kaffe Fassett jersey which she had knitted through the long weeks of her despair. She was as confident and hopeful as it was possible for her to be, considering the circumstances, so got off the train at the station Tom had stipulated with optimism in her heart as well as the inevitable dread.

Tom was waiting on the station forecourt in a red Porsche, which surprised her. He leaned over and opened the passenger door. He had been to see a publisher in Oxford that day, which was why they had not travelled out of London together; Camilla suspected that he had arranged it on purpose. But his greeting was genuinely friendly.

'I dropped Jo on board, and the others are there too, so we'll go straight down to the quay. We have to sail at seven, on the tide. It dries out where she lies.'

Camilla guessed that she wasn't going to cope with the technicalities, so nodded vaguely. And mention of 'the others' was ominous. But zooming along in the Porsche with Tom was lovely. She knew nothing of

Essex, save Ilford and Dagenham, and was surprised to find it distinctly rural. At one point, coming over a rise, there was a glimpse of an estuary ahead, widening rapidly into the distance with an island standing distinct, humped with trees, and the white flecks of yacht sails far out. As the road dropped the view vanished, and it remained in her mind like the image of a dream on waking, a fairy-tale picture. She never expected to be part of a fairy-tale.

They came into an old and pretty town where the barge *Adeline* was moored with several others on the town quay. Tom parked the car in a park some way away and they walked down, Tom carrying her bag, and chatting easily about the place and the barges.

'Nick, the skipper, is a childhood friend of Jo's. He's a real boat bum — you'll see. *Adeline* is his life.'

*Adeline* was magnificent, all one hundred feet of her, with her mast and sprit rearing over the roof of the riverside pub, dark sails brailed and asking to go as the top of the tide sluiced along her black sides. The mooring ropes dipped and hardened with a gentle rhythm.

'Come on!'

The tide was on the turn and introductions

were muddled in a scurry of casting off and making sail, holding on, turning up, bowsing down . . . Camilla was at a complete loss, but pulled where it seemed necessary and kept neatly out of the way of people who seemed to know what they were doing. The activity was short-lived, and as soon as *Adeline* was slipping gently away from the Hythe, freed of her constraints, the chores were left to the three young boys on board who fought each other for the privilege. Nick was on the wheel and more crew was for the present unnecessary. Tom decided it was gin and tonic time, and while he went below with the parents of the keen boys to unearth the ingredients, Camilla was left on deck with Nick and the woman who had occupied her thoughts to a ridiculous degree ever since she had accepted Tom's invitation: Tom's wife.

'Lovely, isn't it?'

Jo had her back turned, watching the town receding over the stern as the barge slid away on the tide at a surprising speed. The town shore of the river was a picturesque jumble of moored boats and old yards and clapboard sheds, behind which the town rose up on its hill, crowned gracefully by a church-tower silhouetted against the setting sun.

'I never get tired of that view, although I've lived here all my life.'

76

Jo turned back to Camilla with a friendly, unaffected smile, and Camilla saw at once that this was not a woman she could dislike. She felt a strange sense of disappointment, that Tom's wife was everything he deserved: warm and bright and generous. She had seen her as an adversary, in spite of the fact that she believed Tom had no interest in her other than as a passing acquaintance. She knew the invitation was a reward, no more. It was hard to see friendship now without strings, without considering the consequences. That was the result of her ten lost years.

'I never get tired of this view either,' Nick said. His view was of *Adeline* before him, her mainsail flowering as the boys released it from its brails. A pungent whiff of old, evocative boat smells came with it, of rope and tar and stale dewstains. Her topsail was already drawing, and with her fresh motive power she started to cream through the water, softly creaking and knocking and groaning as if her grumbles would remind them how venerable she was, relic of a distant age.

To Camilla she was very impressive.

Already she felt a continent away from Covent Garden.

'Nick works on her all the time. She looks a treat, doesn't she?'

Nick put out an arm and gave Jo a brotherly hug.

'You wouldn't think we were at school together, would you? Her a bloody headmistress and all — she always was a right bossy boots.'

Jo laughed and gave him a kiss on the cheek. 'We've both got what we want. We're very lucky.'

'Yeah, well, I never thought I'd ever own one of these, not when I was little, and we used to play on them. Mind you — I don't own much else,' he said to Camilla. 'Not even a decent pair of trousers.'

He certainly gave that impression, being dressed in a paint-splotched boiler-suit, low in the crotch, giving a clownlike impression. He was gaunt and thin, with an amiable smile and dusty-red hair, thick and upstanding, as if it were mowed rather than cut.

'These guys that do up old boats — barges and smacks — they're all fanatics,' Jo said. 'Keeping a barge like this going is like painting the Forth bridge, it's never finished. The more beautiful the boat, the more clapped-out the owner. You can see *Adeline* is very beautiful.'

She laughed.

'You can say that again!' Nick said.

'Drinks coming up!'

A tray of glasses appeared in the hatchway and Tom came out on deck with the parents of the three boys, to whom Camilla was reintroduced, glass in hand, relaxed now, time to take each other in, Ros and Dave. Camilla took care to get the names firmly stuck on, knowing how careless she was with names and faces. It mattered terribly, somehow, that the weekend should go right; she was on such unfamiliar ground — but they were all totally at home, settling down on the deck with their backs against the bulwarks or the sides of the hold, as if there was nothing unusual in taking a gin and tonic under such a spread of sail on a cold spring evening. It was so far removed from the six o'clock swill in London pubs, so utterly unlikely to one unversed in the ways of the sailing fraternity.

'We'll anchor at the mouth of the river. The wind's light, we'll be comfortable enough. That suit you? And go off on the tide in the morning.'

'Breakfast under way?'

'Why not? See what the weather's like.'

'The forecast is good.'

'Where are we going?'

'It's supposed to be a dummy run for the school trip, remember. We're not here to enjoy ourselves! We want a few trips ashore to places of interest, a nice beach or two, with a bit of history thrown in — '

'Nelson sailed out of Harwich — the Medusa buoy is named after his ship,' Nick said. 'He took a passage through the sands that was said to be impossible, and they buoyed it later.'

'That's the sort of thing. I could read up on that. And there are the Martello towers, against an invasion by Napoleon. And we want natural history too — cormorants — '

'They're all over the place.'

'Is she always like this?' Dave asked Tom.

'I'm afraid so.'

'You know it's a working weekend! It's not pleasure!'

'No, we'll have to be careful. We mustn't enjoy it.'

'My God, no. It's for the children.'

'Of course.'

Down the dusking river *Adeline* heeled a fraction to the westerly wind, passing the winking shoal buoys and the island Camilla had seen earlier from the car. She went and stood on the bow and watched the approaching sea, chilled to the bone but eager to take in everything she was being offered. The evening sails had disappeared. A few yachts were moored offshore, a glow of light in their cabin windows, and soon *Adeline*'s sails were taken in again, and she drifted towards the same anchorage under her own way. Timed to a nicety, she met the mudflats and came to an imperceptible halt. Nick put down the anchor. He made it all seem very easy, not hurrying or fussing, yet the craft appeared to Camilla large and unwieldy.

She remarked on this, and he said, 'Not when you know their ways. They were designed to be handled by just one man and his wife, or a man and a boy, that's the beauty of them.'

Camilla could see why Jo thought the barge trip would be a great experience for her children. It was to her, and she on the verge of middle age, who once thought she knew it all.

But the weekend was bad news for Tom. Having asked Camilla out of pure courtesy, he found himself disorientated by her presence, and his mind flying off at wild tangents. He kept thinking of her as a mother figure, the domestic rock in her country cottage, only wanting to cook and tend the fire and mend socks. The picture was in sepia, he was cynical enough to concede, but it would not go away however he rebuked his own sentimentality. How drab she was beside Jo, who was full of energy and delight with the working out of her plans, sparking off ideas and sympathies and programmes of work like fireworks. In her totally right, ancient jeans and faded cotton jersey she looked part of the working scene without affectation, whereas Camilla, steeped in city ways, looked exactly what she was in her beautifully matching but inappropriate sporting separates: out of tune and all at sea, literally. If one wanted to be unkind, she was a bit of a joke. An inland girl, she knew nothing of tides and mudflats, or how sailing worked. She could not hold a candle to Jo, or Ros either for that matter. Yet Tom could not relinquish his notion of Camilla as a mother! Camilla yearning and wasted and unhappy, wanting only one thing to fulfil her, by her own admission. The one thing he too wanted above all else. The three boys on board did not help his idiotic desires, being thoroughly amiable well-brought-up and attractive children, spirited yet polite, funny without having to show off, capable beyond their years.

'They have to be,' Ros said when Nick remarked upon this fact. 'I do two full-time jobs, don't I? I can't do them both properly. They have to fend for themselves — the teaching wins over being a mother, because that's where the money comes from.'

It was as if every remark, every action and presence that weekend was directed solely at his predicament which, in truth, he could not really decide was a real one or imagined. In a sense it made no difference: the rate at which his restlessness was growing alarmed him. He needed the hills and a hundred miles of moorland before him and he might come to terms with what it was that bugged him so, the usual and unfailingly successful method of straightening out the mind.

'I'll go and see my mother next weekend,' he said suddenly to Jo. 'Take a few days off.'

Going to see his mother was a euphemism for going to Wales to walk: he dropped in on the way.

'Very thoughtful,' Jo said, and grinned.

She was going ashore with Camilla and the boys to walk along one of the rare sand beaches on the Essex coast, inaccessible by road. Her enthusiasm was unflagging.

'The naturalists don't come here,' Nick said. 'So it's still in its natural state.'

'Great.'

'I'm opting out,' said Dave. 'Beer on deck for me.'

'I'll join you,' Tom said.

They lay propped against the hatch, watching the barge's tender receding across the water with Nick on the outboard. The sky was clear and milky, the air cool, sparkling — 'Healthy,' Dave said, thinking of the commuter's train in the morning.

'Nick's got something. He'll live to be a hundred. Why do we do what we do?'

'Bread.'

'I wonder sometimes.'

'Don't we all? Except Jo.'

'Ros wants to move back to Norfolk. She's always on at me. Says money's not everything. We're always rowing about it.'

'What would you do up there?' London was the base for Dave's job. He played the cello in a symphony orchestra. Tom couldn't see Ros's argument.

'She says I could teach, play music clubs and suchlike. Can you see me? I'd go nuts. I wish we were in your position.'

'What's my position?'

'Oh, you know, everything you want, no kids to worry about, spend it all on what you like. No eternal rows.'

Tom considered. People were always envying him. His sterile life.

'Everybody wants what they haven't got.'

'That's true.'

After this conversation Tom tried rationally to realise how lucky he was and stop being ridiculous. He ignored Camilla and concentrated on appreciating his lovely Jo, seeing her how other men saw her, not as a stubborn, sterile headmistress, but as a warm, beautiful woman.

'I love you,' he said, testing it out, when they were at home and going to bed. She was full of the weekend's success, flushed by the sun and the wind, full of optimism, excitement even, at the prospect of her school trip.

She flung her arms round him. 'You enjoyed it, didn't you? Everyone did.'

'Not bad.'

'It was lovely. And Nick . . . he's really flowered now he's got *Adeline* actually sailing. All that work!'

Tom kissed her to shut her up. He lay her determinedly on the bed. She shoved at him peevishly.

'Oh, honestly, Tom — '

She wanted to think about everything that was in her head, all the good ideas sprouting; savour the feel of a good weekend while it was still gently glowing, fading, in her mind. Tom could never take her in his arms and comfort, kiss her, lie fondling her and talking, without completing the act. He never kissed her or put his arms round her, only as a prelude to making love. She thought it strange, and a great lack in their relationship. She put it down to his loveless upbringing. His mother was a very unkissing person; she was like a barbed wire fence, and Mr Monk, who, being Gallic, might have been a great kisser, didn't stay around to teach his son much about love.

'What was your father's name? His Christian name?' She gave Tom another shove. He was incredibly strong for a slenderly built man.

'Why do you ask?'

'I'm prevaricating.'

'Alberic.'

Jo found it hard to believe: Alberic Monk. Picturing his spiky mother, Jo knew that Tom was all Alberic Monk, with his intense, nervous eyes and sensitive features. But the upbringing was his mother's. Burning curiosity overtook her.

'You absolutely must find out more about him. When you go, next weekend or whenever — you must. If he's still alive — and why shouldn't he be? — you could arrange to meet him. It's only civilised, after all, to meet your father.'

'If we had a baby, there'd be some point.'

'You should meet him first. He might be the hunchback of Notre Dame. Or an alcoholic. Or a haemophiliac. One should know about these things.'

'If I found out, if I met him, then you'd have a baby?'

'No!'

She flung herself away violently, her face contorting. 'Why do you have to spoil it? You know what I feel about it! Why do you have to spoil a lovely weekend — such a lovely weekend!'

He got up abruptly. Fastening his clothes quickly, he reached for the jersey he had thrown off earlier and went out of the room. Jo heard the front door slam.

She turned over on the rumpled bed and wept into the pillow.

# 3

At the next governors' meeting, Jo put forward her idea of taking twelve children on the barge trip during the summer halfterm. She was not asking permission, but stating a fact.

She saw the governor who was Lorna and Crispin Grott's neighbour and buddy adjust her face to a non-committal expression. Ann Forrester's face was normally aglitter with greed for information, for gossip and scandal; she had loud opinions and was clever, which made her habit of enquiring deeply into all decisions dangerous as well as extremely tedious. She was the mother of a stolid nine-year-old son and an elfin five-year-old daughter who as yet showed none of their mother's snakelike attributes. The fact that she was fairly obviously loathed by the other nine governors apparently did not weigh with her; she had a steel shell.

No doubt primed by Grott, she asked, 'I'm a bit concerned about safety. Can you tell us what provisions you are taking as to safety?'

'Are you not familiar with the Thames barge?'

'No, I'm not.' Mrs Forrester smiled blandly, when any lesser body would have felt at a disadvantage. 'I take it they are very safe?'

'A child would have difficulty falling over the side. It would have to climb over. The barge we are going on has a Board of Trade certificate of seaworthiness, and a professional skipper.'

'Are any other teachers going?'

'One other, and I'm taking Stevie to help. He has volunteered.'

'Ah, Stevie,' said Mrs Forrester thoughtfully.

Jo held her breath in case the wretched woman should go off at a tangent on the subject of Stevie, reiterating Crispin's grudges, but benevolent Dr Frost put in his word.

'It seems to me an admirable project, with great gain to the lucky children who are able to go along. I think we should be very grateful that Mrs Monk is willing to provide this sort of adventure for the children during her own holiday time.'

'Mrs Monk does indeed think up very good holiday ideas, usually ideas in which she herself holds a great interest,' Mrs Forrester said pointedly. She was referring to a ski trip Jo had inaugurated the year before. 'Can I ask what the barge will cost per child and whether the whole cost will be borne by the children concerned?'

Jo gave her the sums. 'I will of course be paying my own expenses out of my salary.'

'This time — ah, good.'

Jo found herself tightening her lips to stop herself letting rip at Forrester like a fishwife, and was saved by a broad wink of amusement from a councillor across the table. The meeting was running overtime; it was seven o'clock and Tom would be home. Who would have put the baby to bed, for God's sake, if he had his way? Tomorrow being Friday he was off to Wales and his mother en route, and the fraught week between them would hopefully be forgotten when he returned home in a refreshed frame of mind. Or was his condition now permanent? Jo was unhappy with the home front. Tom lay unmoving on his side of the bed and the only time she had made a conciliatory move towards love-making he had said, 'There's really no point in it, the way you feel about things.'

'It's my life too.'

Work had never been more rewarding. Her clutch of children ready and primed for going up into the secondary school in the autumn had been commented upon very favourably by the secondary headmaster when they had made their preliminary visits; she had had enthusiastic praise from the inspectorate and the Friends of the School had given her a very large record token 'in appreciation of everything you do beyond the call of duty' — an unexpected and touching gesture. Ann Forrester was not a Friend of the School. If I have a baby, Jo thought, she will make sure Crispin stands in for me. She always got herself on to the interview panel. She had been Crispin's champion for Deputy, against considerable opposition. She did not mind having her back to the wall, and talking, talking, wearing more amenable colleagues away, impervious to vibrations of hostility. Possibly she did not recognise them, or was used to them from childhood. Jo could see her a schoolgirl, bossy and insensitive, whining into favour, manipulating friendships. She was married to a pale-faced, mostly silent solicitor who stayed late at the office. He rarely came to the Parents' meetings or to concerts or sports days. But once Jo had seen him riding his daughter's tiny bicycle down the road, wearing only shorts and an eye-shade, the child screaming with laughter on the pavement. She did not know enough to judge him, but pitied him his wife.

When she got home Tom was making his

own meal, cooking something for one in the microwave.

'What is it? Is there another? I'm famished.' But he made no move to look for another packet and she had to do it herself. He hated her not being at home when he came in, which was late enough usually. The atmosphere was cold. How bloody unfair life was, Jo thought. She did her best by everyone, and all she got for her trouble was a guilt complex like a Sherpa's rucksack on her shoulders. But Tom had a conviction that 'everyone does exactly what they want to do in this life'. It was impossible to plead her cause with him. He was probably right.

He departed the following morning with his sleeping bag and boots in the back of the car and said, 'I'll ring you. I'll take three or four days — back Tuesday night, most likely. Wednesday perhaps.'

'Give my regards to your mother.'

He grunted.

Jo had a feeling that decisions were to be made.

When he had gone she busied herself with sorting out the letters she had had back from her parents about the barge trip. There were far too many wanting to come and she was going to have to arrange another later, and this encouragement sustained her. She did not dare to contemplate her domestic situation.

★   ★   ★

Tom drove down the M4 to Wiltshire in the outer lane, trying not to be a bully but failing, because of the neurotic anger that surfaced so readily. He planned to walk the Carnedds, spend a night under a wall on the tops somewhere with the stars close and the cold earth damping the fires of unreason.

But first his duty call, and a night in the fourposter of Lord Rammington's guest room. The stately home where his mother worked was in the last stages of decrepitude, like its owner, but none the less beautiful for its decay: more so, in fact, there being an indisputable romance about beauty in decay. The Victorian painters loved it, dab hands at swags of ivy hanging from Gothic walls. Going to the Rammington's pile, called dully Parklands, was not entirely a chore, for Tom had come to love the unfolding of the buildings in all their glorious disarray as the long drive of limes curved gradually to disclose them. The limes were very old, dying in parts. The grass was kept mowed on either side by the single gardener/groom/handyman James, aged seventy-three, just enough to spark a welcome for the treat ahead, the sprawling Elizabethan house with its Georgian front and long-locked grandiose doors above a double flight of steps. The first time Tom had called he had gone in at the front doors, finding them open, and had discovered himself in a magnificent pillared hall, big as a ballroom. In one corner, huddled in a tartan rug, Lord Rammington had been watching the Irish — Scottish rugger final on the television, shouting spasmodically and spilling his whisky. The hall, apart from his Lordship's television, had been quite bare. Lately it had been locked up, and only a small wing of the house was used now, at the back. The deterioration of the place was caused not by lack of money but by apathy, the heir to the place being a grandson who was a playboy and a heroin addict. Rammington was now very elderly and his needs were catered for by a cook and a housekeeper, Tom's mother Elizabeth. Elizabeth ran the place, although she had been hired originally to run the stud which had in the past produced many winners. It now ticked over, paying its way, and it was still Elizabeth's prime interest. After a racketty life she had found in Parklands a perfect satisfaction. Tom wondered whether her life would be shattered again when Rammington died or whether he was going to provide some sort of continuity for her. It was hard to see how. But Tom knew his mother would never look to him for help.

It was she who ordered the place, concentrating the efforts of the skeleton staff. The parks were kept grazed by neighbours' cattle which were also used for cleaning off the magnificent stud paddocks. The ancient stables were entered through an archway under a clock-tower. The few — but priceless — mares came to the open top-doors as he drove in, and Tom found his mother putting away the halters in the tack-room.

'I've timed it well?'

'Yes.'

They never enthused on meeting, or kissed.

Tom was relieved he did not have to sit around waiting while she filled feed buckets or picked out hooves. She was ready to come up to the house.

'All going well?'

'In the stables, yes. In the house we are deteriorating, I'm afraid. The antics of our young heir do nothing to help.'

'What's he up to now?'

'He's in custody. He gave a party that was raided by the police, and they were all on heroin, of course. The newspapers will have a field day when it comes to court.'

It seemed very strange, to be heir to such a

paradise as Parklands, and wilfully eschew it. There was no shortage of money for the upkeep, only a lack of will, and bitter disappointment in the old man. His own son, father of the addict, had been killed in a plane crash, having had three wives first (but only one child). Wealth, in this case, had not brought happiness.

Tom was not sentimental but the old house always gave him a wrench of nostalgia, as if he were a born-again Elizabethan, as if he had known these pared-down gardens in their herbaceous heyday, was familiar with table talk about Cranmer or the succession and with riding his horse out of the park towards Salisbury. The house was rooted on the face of England, faded brick and facing stone and winks of thick Tudor glass gazing out across now brief lawns and overgrown avenues. The avenues came from four directions, but only the one from the road was mowed. Rooks wheeled over the topmost branches as they went up from the yard across the back lawn. The classic design of the house in the garden was still beautiful in neglect, as a face can be beautiful from its bone structure alone, and Tom could see that his austere mother somehow perfectly fitted this setting. And yet her tenure here was fragile, depending on the ancient owner.

'So how is the old man?'

'Tired. Very frail. You'll see.'

Formality still prevailed, and Tom when he visited was always asked to dinner. His mother ate with Rammington in the evening and they were waited on by the cook-cum-housekeeper, Gladys, a widow who came and went each day in an ancient Cortina. For Gladys's sake they ate early; she liked to be home in time for 'The Eastenders'.

'You go and have a drink with him now, while I have a wash, and then we can talk after dinner. He always falls asleep over the television — we'll be alone.'

She could have been his wife, the way it was. Tom made his way to the dining-room and found Lord Rammington sitting in front of the fire. The fireplace was the original Tudor; the burning logs, large enough by normal standards, nowhere near filled it, but made a cheerful picture to Tom, attuned to central heating. An ancient retriever slumbered on a threadbare hearthrug and horses, far more ancient, stared down from the walls, their shining coats now dulled with wood-smoke and age.

'Tom?'

'Don't get up, sir.'

Tom came forward hastily to shake hands as Rammington fumbled dangerously with his whisky glass.

'Help yourself, will you? Nice to see you again.'

Yes, he was frail, transparent almost, the bony hands webbed with swollen veins, trembling on the glass. He had an impressive past, had served in two wars, and on countless committees and enquiries into upright subjects, was known for his sportsmanship and integrity and humanity; had also loved and played strenuously. He had outlived all his friends and companions and now spent all day slowly, with fierce independence, going through the laborious procedures of existence — getting himself up, which took almost all morning, and in the evening reversing the process, too exhausted in between to do more than doze and dream and shed the pages of the *Daily Telegraph* over the floor.

'I've overlived my time,' he would say, and his great strength and capacity for living was now his burden.

Tom, seeing all this as they chatted, was strongly aware of the junkie grandson. The old man was still alert in his conversation. Henry was not mentioned, but Tom sensed that Rammington was covering — by his very brightness — a bitter disappointment. His life had been steered by an old-fashioned, now largely outmoded, sense of duty to God and country, service before self. The grandson had spent his youth learning that he had never had it so good, that to express one's self was the purpose of life. They were both extreme products of their age. Most people managed to steer a path through batty excesses, but neither of these two men could remotely overlap each other's ground. It was more than a generation gap. It was an abyss. He should have died ten years ago, Tom thought, before Henry was found out.

'And how is it with you? How are the children?'

'There aren't any, I'm afraid.'

'Lord, sorry. I forget everything these days. Don't tell Elizabeth I thought she was a grandmother!'

He was so gentlemanly, so careful of not hurting other's susceptibilities, turning his mistakes into a small joke, so desperately hurt himself. Tom could see the change in him, and wondered if he hid his own disappointment as successfully. What a pair they made, the man who wanted a child above all else, and the man who had and no doubt wished he hadn't — what a toss-up it was, these caprices of nature, this jangling of the genes, thrown into the whirlpool to sink or swim ... The whisky on an empty stomach was getting at Tom, and he was glad when his mother arrived and Gladys came in with the dinner. But he felt well-primed to accost his mother later, on his parentage. The path was well-laid. He ensured that he drank exactly the right amount of Rammington's very good Beaujolais to keep his nerves at the correct pitch, highly but not over tuned, his tongue loosened just enough. His mother drank hardly at all, as always. Like most outdoor people, she seemed to stay at the same age over many years, only the colour of the eyes fading, and the blonde hair greying almost imperceptibly, the tone the same but the brightness gone. She was stiff only in her manner, which had always been her way, not speaking easily in company. Her own parents had been hunting people from the shires, well off ('Well orff,' Jo mocked) but over bossy. A secretive, only child, she had left home early and never returned, and her parents had died comparatively young without grieving her much. She was her own person, and formidable as mothers went. Tom, by the time the dinner was over, was in a rare state of anticipation for more family history.

The table was large and they sat one on each side, his lordship at the head, talking loudly across the gaps. There was room for a dozen at least, and the shining mahogany laid for three with the finest silver and glasses. Tom understood that it was always like this, even with just the two of them. His mother, although clean and brushed, had not changed, and her old cords and woollen shirt gave off the faintest odour of horse. Time to change would have to be cut from time in the stables, and that was at a premium. It suited her to have Tom call at the rarest possible intervals and Jo had learned quickly that there was no spare time for tedious family get-togethers. In that, Jo was similar. These women dedicated to their work . . . mothering did not run in them. It occurred to Tom then that he must have been a mistake. His pulse ran a little faster. He — that important being, Tom Monk — a mistake, one of nature's innumerable tricks! He stopped drinking, afraid he was on the verge of having too much.

'You two stay and have coffee here by the fire. I'm going to watch 'Panorama' and then to bed. Goodnight, Tom old chap, it's good to see you again.'

Tom got up and shook hands again, and thanked him, and the old boy shambled with difficulty, leaning on his stick, out of the room.

Gladys brought the coffee, plonking it down on the table, and bade them goodnight.

In a moment they heard her car start up and drive away.

'Doesn't she wash up?'

'I put it in the dishwasher, it's no trouble. Shall we take it over to the fire? There's a small table somewhere.'

Tom found it and put it athwart the dog and Elizabeth brought the tray. She put some more logs on the fire.

'I take it you're off to Wales?'

'Yes.'

'Jo never wants to go?'

'No, she's too wrapped up in her work.'

'It's not everybody's idea of a holiday, I suppose. Although she's very active.'

'Walking's for thinking.'

'Is it? But you think for a living. For a holiday too?'

'Another sort of thinking.' He was talking like a child.

There was a long silence while he contemplated the vital questions, but before he could frame the first his mother started to talk at some length — for her — of her problems with a certain very valuable mare. Tom made a show of listening, but Rammington's alcohol was now coursing in the bloodstream, and as the fresh logs began to spit and flare his uncertainties pressed more strongly.

'It's finding the right bloodline to niche in with our own — I can never be sure if it's a science or pure luck, but one does one's best by the theory.'

'I wanted to talk to you about bloodlines. Mine actually.'

'Whatever do you mean?'

'My father. I'm curious.'

'After all these years?' She smiled. 'You never were. What's changed?'

'I want to have a family. It seems logical to be curious in the circumstances — like you were saying, about blood-lines.'

'All perfectly healthy, my dear, to the best of my knowledge. He was extremely wellbred, had exquisite manners, a fascinating face, a lot of charm — oh, how I loved him!'

'Why didn't you marry him?'

'He was already, in a sense, married.'

'In what sense?'

'To the church. Have you never wondered about your name?'

Tom wondered now. The alcohol raced strangely, its heat flaring across his cheek-bones.

'Monk? The surname, you mean?'

'It wasn't his name. It was his profession.'

All the other questions Tom had prepared sank into oblivion at this stunning remark. His mother watched the evidence of his shock with sympathy.

'You see why I never wanted to talk about it? It was too difficult a subject. In the early days I was afraid, but now, after all this time, it seems merely absurd. He was a French monk who came over to England on a retreat. After he met me, I turned into the retreat. He came every year for a few years, for his soul, he said. For his body, in truth.'

'How could he?' Tom was deeply, unashamedly, shocked.

'Well, he was French.'

'What was his real name?'

'Alberic.'

'Alberic what? What's his real surname?'

'Barbier. Alberic Barbier.'

'That's a rose!'

'A rose? Perhaps I've made a mistake. No, that's what he told me.'

'He lied! It was a joke!'

'No, Tom. It wasn't a joke at all. When he discovered I was pregnant he said, 'C'est la vie,' and went home. He never came on a retreat again.'

'He left you?'

'Well, you can't call it leaving. We were never together, were we? Only in the fields below the monastery walls. It was all very beautiful, Tom. Don't spoil it by being prudish and intolerant. He did truly love me, and I him, but of course it was all a terrible mistake. I worked in a stable near the monastery, you see, and we used to see each other over the wall when I rode past. You can always see into gardens when you are riding — it's surprising, sometimes, what you see. The weather was so lovely, and he supposed to be meditating . . . in his great, hot habit. It was against nature.'

Tom couldn't begin to remonstrate. It was all far and away beyond what he had expected. His mother fetched him a brandy from his Lordship's stock, and he was grateful.

He sat staring into the fire. He, so cool, so Londonish, so altogether (he thought) was as outraged as a Victorian spinster. His hand was shaking on his glass just like old Rammington's.

'I would have thought you might be rather pleased,' his mother said presently. 'It's different, at least. More style than a butcher, say, or a motor mechanic. What were you hoping for?'

What indeed? He had asked through a sense of responsibility, a characteristic he had not inherited from his father. It was Jo who had been curious and set him off.

'It was never sordid, Tom. Not like the back of a car. It was very beautiful, in the water-meadows. You were a true love-child.'

'You couldn't have wanted me?'

'Not at the time, but I wouldn't give you up. I didn't have you adopted. I did my best by you and you didn't have an unhappy childhood as childhoods go.'

It was true that he had never felt deprived, his mother's way of life being interesting to a child: living in large country places where she worked as groom/housekeeper or housekeeper/ groom or filled the requirements 'must be good with children and dogs, clean driving license'. Mostly friendly families and other children around, although very often cold quarters and a long way to school. Single mothers were already in fashion and nobody ever enquired as to his father. His mother wanting him so much — nearly always nice to him, and patient — had given the vital security. Perhaps if Jo had a child under duress, her resentment would in some way express itself in the child. 'I want a child so badly, but Jo doesn't want one. I don't know what to do about it.'

'Oh, women are like that today, I'm afraid,' his mother said vaguely. 'They've their own lives to lead.'

'You didn't want me, but you were glad you had me afterwards?'

'Yes.'

'I tell Jo it's like that, you always love them when they come, even if you don't want them.'

'It might not work for Jo. There are no rules. My mother, for example, could never be bothered with me. She was furious when she had to stay at home to look after me instead of going hunting. She told me what a bore I was. I can remember. When I had you I knew I would never let you feel like that, it was so awful.'

Hearing about his parentage, however weird, increased the desire in Tom to be a father. No one could say his lineage was dull, whatever else. After a deep and dreamless night in the fourposter, he drove away in the morning down the ancient avenue, with a parting question.

'What order was he in?'

'Benedictine.'

His mother stood waving until the curve of the drive hid her, and Tom thought again what a monstrous problem he was making of something so casual in life, the making of it, done under hedges and in back alleys all over the country. When these trees were planted, girls were lifting their skirts in the cow parsley to men in doublet and hose (how difficult) and no contraception beyond jumping off the cow-byre roof or taking a concoction of emetic herbs. If he had a son he could call it Ben.

★   ★   ★

Elizabeth's conversation with Tom set in train a wave of remembrance, bringing back details she had long forgotten. Strongest was a passionate longing for those naked monk-pale arms to take her body to its own in the way that had produced Tom. Such ecstasy of loving one was lucky to have known at all, even fleetingly — better than a lifetime of worthy marriage without fire. Elizabeth had never wanted to share her life with anyone, but the unnannounced, spasmodic appearances of her French lover over a period of four years had entranced her and now, thirty years on, she felt, after the reminiscing, a stronger sense of loss than she could remember feeling at the time. Then at twenty, she had hoped that such love would come again, or that her monk might eventually return, unfrocked, to claim her. But life wasn't like that. Those ecstasies had been her ration, and she had grown hard and leathery with the frosting of her biological needs. No other man had interested her although several had tried to sortie into her Siberian regions, without success. No other man she had ever looked at had produced the thrill that the monk's deep-set, dark and passionate gaze had aroused in her. The accompanying flow of French she had not understood, nor wished to. She had tied her horse to a willow tree and in the cool grasses by the swiftly-flowing River Avon jodhpurs and habit had been abandoned and untried bodies joined, with only the sound of distant cuckoos and plopping trout to accompany their union. What beginners' luck! The instinctive coupling transcended ignorance. After a lifetime with recalcitrant mares meeting stallions, Elizabeth was still amazed at her own success in the mating field — and she so angular and asexual, all fine bones and taut sinews, breasts scarcely formed, thighs hard as sapling trunks with endless riding. How bored he must have been in the Benedictine fastnesses, to generate such fire in directions so far from God! Did he confess to a fascinated superior? She never knew. At the time it had been a living fairy-story, even to the reality of his dropping down over the wall on to the back of her horse and her riding away over the flowering meadows with his arms round her waist.

She could not help laughing at the memory of it. The naivety of their affair, the simplicity of the commitment, astonished her in jaded middle age. She was full of admiration for her young self. Coupling today seemed so sordid, sparked off by loud disco music and too much to drink, achieved in supermarket car-parks at night, in laybys and on sofas with the television still turned on. Or was she being unjust? The Tudor maids no doubt had equally as hurried unions in byre and bakery. Through history the lust of youth had expressed itself more in haste than with taste. She herself had been conceived (according to her mother) in the back of a horsebox (an early model) between the Novice and Open classes at the local show. (Her mother had competed in both.)

Elizabeth recalled Tom's stunned expression and laughed out loud. She was holding a mare for the vet at the time. His arm was deep into the mare's vagina and the mare had an expression of supreme boredom on her face, as well she might. The sordid operations bore no relation to the animals' wild cavorting in the do-it-yourself situation; the poor animals were too valuable to be left to their own devices, but must be primed and hobbled and helped.

'What's so funny?' grumbled the vet.

Elizabeth did not reply.

Tom was so funny really . . . if only he knew how, every time she spoke to him, she was bemused by his likeness to his father: those dark and mysterious eyes, all secrets with Tom, the loose-jointed athletic grace (how his father had swung over the wall! — really quite high). His reserve and dislike of talking much he took from her, poor fellow, for Alberic had been a great talker, even though she did not understand — well, the gist of it was clear enough. Were Benedictines the ones that didn't talk? Perhaps he was just making up for it.

Funny too how earnest he was about having a child. In her family babies had been not wanted but stoically accepted when they came. But now Jo presumably was cleverly preventing it all happening. Elizabeth did not like Jo. She suspected her dislike was possibly a touch of the notorious mother-in-law sour grapes, for Jo had this admirable capacity for making her attitudes absolutely clear, no secrets about Jo; she laughed a lot and had a huge and active enjoyment of all she did. She was totally nice. But she jarred on Elizabeth. If Jo did not want a baby she had no doubt made this quite clear to Tom.

Poor Tom. If it mattered so much he would have to find another, run two homes even, very French, like his father.

Elizabeth knew that Rammington was

going to leave her a good deal of money when he died, for he had discussed it with her and it was in his will. She did not want money, not that much. She wasn't used to it and work was her life. She would tell Tom about it and tell him he could have it if he wanted. She too would like Tom to have a child. The idea of perpetuating Alberic Barbier enchanted her. If it was a girl he could call it Rose.

★ ★ ★

It took Tom seventy-three miles to come to terms with being fathered by a monk, and the inclination to continue this rare line hardened with every step he took. Sleeping under a wall on the top of Cernedd Llewelyn, the stars apparently as close as the lights away on Anglesey across the black dark of the bay, he dreamed of a child in a monk's habit, whisking through summer fields, looking just like the boy he had met on the seawall that evening with Jo. Perhaps the romantic connection would change Jo's mind. He would try it out on her as soon as he got back.

It didn't.

Instead of prevaricating, she was forced by his insistence to make a decision. She said no.

'What difference does it make?'

She had no imagination. She was frightened, but her mind was made up.

'I've thought about it a lot. It wouldn't be fair on the child, the way I feel.'

Tom argued, inevitably. All the same old arguments, but for the last time.

'Can't you accept it? It's worked so well, just the two of us.'

Jo's face was bleak.

'I do love you, Tom. It's nothing to do with not loving you, you know that. I suppose there's something wrong with me, but I can't help it.'

For better or worse, the situation was resolving itself. What had once been a muddle was now a clearcut situation.

'You won't leave me? I suppose it's grounds.' She spoke quietly, with resignation, as if she thought he would.

'No. I won't leave you. It doesn't matter.'

'You're lying.'

'Well . . . I won't leave you. That's not a lie.'

Two days later his mother's letter came, telling him that she wanted him to have Rammington's money.

'It's of no use to me. Think of it as a present from Henry, to stop him killing himself — the old man has cut him out of his will. I am sure you can use it more usefully than I can. I doubt if the poor fellow will last more than a couple of years at the rate he is declining.'

Tom read this letter in the train going to work. It was amazing the way it set his imagination to work. He was still sitting in a dream at Liverpool Street after all the commuters had got out and the porter was coming along slamming the doors. He scrambled himself together.

The sun was shining in Bishopsgate and he set off walking for Cheapside, humming a tune.

# 4

'I'm going to swim to the other side. I can
— I'll show you!'

'Are you sure, Daniel?'

'I've swum the same distance keeping by
the bank, honest, mum. I know I can.'

Liz hadn't the heart to deter him. She
should do it. But she wasn't a marvellous
swimmer and if he sank before he reached the
far bank she wasn't going to be in much of a
position to help him. This is where she missed
Pete so. He had been a splendid swimmer.

But life was all about taking considered
risks, in Liz's opinion.

'Okay, yes, I'm sure you'll find it no
problem. Have a little rest before you start
back.'

'I'll show you!'

He was thin and brown, all joints and
eagerness, growing fast. Liz watched proudly,
nervously as he plunged in off the salting and
struck out with his rapid, splashy stroke for
the mudbank opposite. The water was
freezing by her standards; it was only May
and there had been little sunshine, but it
didn't put him off. She hadn't been in yet,

but always came down to keep an eye on him. There was rarely anyone around, only dog walkers and the odd jogger.

But today, just as Daniel reached the far bank and she stood up to cheer, two more boys appeared over the wall, and stripped off to swim. They were much the same age as Daniel and jiggered on the bank for a while, then wrestled each other into the water with loud screams. They seemed to have no one to look after them, and were not proficient enough, it seemed to Liz, to be unsupervised.

Having satisfied herself that Daniel was safely, strongly, on his way back, she watched the two newcomers anxiously. Whether she liked it or not she felt herself responsible for them too. They screamed a lot. If they actually came to drowning, it would be difficult to tell. She moved along the bank towards them, annoyed at both them and herself.

'Do your parents know you're swimming down here?' she called to the nearest one. He returned her query by calling her a nosy old cow.

'Ma, did you see me?'

Daniel was standing up now, demanding congratulations. She returned to him with relief.

'That was great, really great! You've come on splendidly!'

He climbed out, grabbing at the sea lavender, juddering with cold and excitement. She wrapped the towel round him.

'Do you know those two boys?'

'Yes, they're in my class. Kevin Tranter and Mark Smith.'

She left him to dry himself. The two boys' language fouled the spring evening, angering her. She would not put herself in a position to be abused again, but felt bound to stay until they had finished, in case they needed help.

They didn't.

'I fuss,' she thought. But decided to tell Mrs Monk of her anxieties. Mesdames Tranter and Smith possibly had no idea where their sons were.

But on later occasions they came again, still unsupervised, and told her it was none of her business, so she shut her mind to it. It was good for young boys to roam free and not be namby-pambyed. All the same, even if she was a fusser, she would never let Dan swim by himself.

As a matter of routine, Jo contacted the Tranter and Smith parents and asked if they knew that their sons were swimming in the creek. Yes, they knew. Jo said as long as they knew, fine; she assumed they were capable swimmers, to be allowed to swim without supervision? Well, we think so, said the Smiths. Good. Mr Tranter said he thought so too and added a rider to the effect that she was a nosy old cow, similar to his son's remark to Liz Weston. Jo put the phone down without comment, angry, and at the same time wondering if she was catching the Grott mentality. Pastoral care, the bane of the schoolteacher, was catching up with her. The Tranter and Smith parents knew perfectly well what their children were up to, as good parents should. It was natural for Tranter senior to resent the implication that he was a careless parent. He was an aggressive character who spoke his mind, unlike the easy-going Smiths. He had put Kevin down for her barge trip and if the boy was excluded Jo knew he would be round to find out the reasons why. Jo knew she would include Kevin, although he was not a model child, being disobedient, rude and sometimes dishonest, but life would be easier for her if she avoided a confrontation with the parents. Aggressive people got their way over the meek precisely for such reasons. It was very hard not to show favouritism. Daniel Weston was a favourite, as Kevin Tranter was not, but because Jo knew she would not refuse Daniel a place, it mattered more to include the less lovable. In truth it could be argued that the trip would be more useful to the rude, the disobedient and the selfish, because the sea was a great leveller and could well teach them a thing or two.

And while Jo was preoccupied with such matters, Tom, without feeling that he was committing himself, initiated a gentle wooing of Camilla. He first approached her after a concert in the church and suggested they have a coffee together (not church coffee) before returning to work. He later asked her to a recital at the Wigmore Hall. To himself he said he was getting to know her better, eschewing the idea that it could be as a prospective mother to his child. He would not admit it. Yet he knew he had no other motive in being disloyal to Jo. He knew that a man who lied to himself was the biggest deceiver of the lot. He knew he was a shit. He got it from his father.

Camilla was patently in love with him. Not a man of great self-regard (one of his better qualities) he could not be blind to this fact. He would rather it was otherwise; he would have preferred a more cerebral commitment, a cool appraisal of what he was offering (what indeed? He wasn't sure himself) but he knew by Camilla's manner that her thoughts were anything but cool. She was gauche with love, with sudden darts of bright colour, with fumbling embarrassment at a protective arm across a busy street. Tom could not return this awakening, but he was by no means unmoved by Camilla. She intrigued him. When he had left her he looked forward to seeing her again, soon. He was on the verge of falling in love, but had sold the condition to himself, and knew perfectly well that if circumstances dictated he could stop quite easily. He was not proud of himself or even sure that he was doing the right thing but, like his father, he decided to use opportunities as they arose. Like the church to his father, so was Jo to him, solid as a rock. But the church was not all.

He told Jo he was going to the Wigmore Hall and she presumed he was going alone. He met Camilla in the foyer at seven o'clock and bought her a drink in the bar, then went into the hall. Tom loved this hall, which he always felt was a victim of time-warp, with its Edwardian standard lamp standing guard over the grand piano, its red plush seats, dark panelling and polished brass.

'I love this hall,' Camilla said.

'Yes, so do I.'

'I hate the Barbican.'

'Yes. But the Festival Hall's all right.'

'Yes.'

The trouble with Camilla was that conversation with her was less than scintillating, unless one got into something very deep. She had very little small talk. Tom thought he ought to kiss her tonight. He had got about far enough, he thought, without. The programme was romantic — Chopin and Schumann and Liszt — and should leave them in the right frame of mind. He felt excited, like a small boy. He could quite see why people had affairs purely out of boredom. Even pretending to be in love was quite exciting.

The woman who played the piano wore white satin and pearls. She had a name that had been around for a bit, British and plain. She wasn't a Russian whizz-kid or Asian inscrutable, but a scrubbed-looking public schoolgirl with big arms and wide bottom. To Tom's surprise she played like an angel, strongly, accurately and with great feeling. He had expected to mildly enjoy the concert, but he enjoyed it enormously, and came out at the end feeling uplifted and full of optimism. Great passion had raged in the large British bosom, not worn on the sleeve; it was refreshing and far more interesting.

Outside, the evening was mild and springlike, not yet properly dark.

'We can walk?' Tom suggested. 'You're not

too far from here — I can get the tube from Covent Garden.'

'It'll make you late.'

'It doesn't matter.' He felt quite reckless.

'Does Jo know you're with me?'

Typical of her, Camilla had to bring up the one thing best left unsaid.

'No, she doesn't. Does it make a difference?'

'Yes, of course it makes a difference.'

'I don't want to talk about it, not now.' He tried to make the brusque words kindly.

'I just want to know where I am.'

'In Wigmore Street, coming up to Cavendish Square.'

'No — '

'I'm sorry. I can't tell you. It's impossible.'

She seemed to accept that. It was as well the situation was made clear, although he had shied away from it; in fact he felt better for being recognised as the errant male. She did not say any more and they walked across Oxford Street and through Soho in companionable silence. They turned down Neal Street, close now to where Camilla lived, and Tom reached for her hand. It was cold and bony, but gripped his tightly like a child's. He felt an adolescent excitement coursing through his bloodstream, quite unlike anything he now felt for Jo. When they got to the door of her flat she said, 'I can't ask you up, not with Auntie. She's so boring.'

'No, it doesn't matter. I've enjoyed it. Do you want to do it again some time?'

'Yes, I do.'

'I'm glad. I'll see you in the church on Thursday and we'll plan something.'

'Yes. Goodbye then.'

She did not turn away for the door, but held her face up to his. He kissed her, at first tentative, then, as she responded so eagerly, with delicious excitement. It was amazing, 'a whole new ball-game' as Terry would have said. So different from Jo. He had somehow expected it to be a duty but, Camilla, like the pianist, harboured passions not apparent in her appearance.

As he sat in the train going home he knew that this tentative exploring of possibilities had landed him in a situation he had not at all foreseen. Why, with hindsight, he could not imagine. But he felt fantastic: biology was winning over logic, such was nature's way. All the symptoms of being in love possessed him. He felt like a youth again. He felt as his father must have done when he leapt over the wall. Homo sapiens, he presumed, was never intended to be monogamous. Nature had to proceed, and that was what he was about.

★ ★ ★

Loving Camilla was quite different from loving Jo, but Tom's love for Jo did not grow any the less. He discovered that he could love two women without any trouble. His moodiness towards Jo, for having made the decision not to bear him a child, dissolved now that he saw the alternative possibility. With his newfound youth he loved her all the more. Jo bloomed with his new cheerfulness and his apparent abandonment of the late obsession about babies. Love begat love, so it seemed. Life was never more satisfactory.

Tom took Camilla to another evening concert, at the Barbican this time, and in the interval, having a drink in the usual crush, Camilla said, 'Our choir at church has been invited to sing in the Berlioz Requiem in Ely Cathedral. The last Saturday in May.'

'That thing with four brass bands, a vast orchestra, six choirs and a trombone blowing raspberries?'

''La Grande Messe des Morts', yes. Four choirs actually. Two hundred voices or thereabouts. I thought you might like to come up?'

'Yes, I would.'

'We're going in a coach. There'd be room for you.'

'And going back afterwards? It's quite a way.'

'Yes. You'd be very late home, I'm afraid.'

During the rest of the concert Tom's mind was occupied with working out whether the trip to Ely could be turned into the obvious 'dirty weekend'. Mozart helped him to visualise it in the fairest of lights. He could take her up in the Porsche and after the concert a hotel somewhere . . . not Ely — some of the others might be staying there. Newmarket possibly, an anonymous sort of place like the Moat House . . . but how could he explain his absence to Jo? There was no way he could be going to see a client over a weekend. The only possibility might be to say he was going to walk the Ridgeway or some other innocuous home counties ramble, but he would be so obviously unweathered when he got home it would be difficult to deceive her.

However, as if it were meant by God, Jo announced a week before the concert that she was going on a weekend conference to discuss the propositions in the new Education bill, exams at seven years old, which she patently disapproved of. She would be far too wrapped up in her own affairs to give much thought to his, and when he said he might go up to Ely for the Requiem — 'It's very rarely performed, and it might be quite something played in a cathedral' — she agreed that it was a good idea.

'I'll stay up there if you're all tied up — I've always been curious about the fen country — wouldn't mind having a nose round before I come home.'

'Okay, that'll suit me.'

She didn't connect Camilla with concert-going, having forgotten that they met because Camilla recognised him from the choir connection. Tom had always been in the habit of going to concerts alone. Jo was bored by classical music. As far as she was concerned Camilla had been invited for the barge weekend to pay back a kindness and dropped thereafter.

Tom put the proposition to Camilla two days before they were due to go.

'If you agree, I can book us in at the hotel.'

He felt distinctly nervous, not at all the suave adulterer.

Camilla did not answer at once. They were sitting outside their lunchtime church, on the same bench where he had first seen her crying. The sun soaked into the old stone behind them; the smell of the traffic mingled uneasily with the powerful spring scent of a late fading lilac that grew precariously amongst the stone memorials, and the hum and muted roar of the City was like a cocoon around them. Beyond the gate strings of lunchtime City men and typing temps hurried past, and two middle-aged ladies up from the suburbs came to read the ancient gravestones, seeking culture now they were freed from the ties of their children. 'Like an oasis,' said one of them appreciatively. They sat on the other seat to rest their ankles. Tom watched them, waiting for his answer.

'It's Jo,' Camilla said uncertainly.

'She won't know. She's at a conference for the weekend.'

'I don't like lies. Deceit. It's sordid.'

'If she actually asked me, I wouldn't lie to her. I'd tell her. But she's so occupied with her work she doesn't ask me. Does that make it better?'

'Why do you want me when you've got Jo?'

He could hardly say that he was testing her out for motherhood. If she had remembered their first conversation on the night of the mugging she might realise.

'Why do you ask unanswerable questions?' he countered.

'You do love Jo, don't you?'

'Yes.'

God, she was awkward! 'It's not uncommon, to be attracted to another person when

127

you're already married.' The evidence was there in abundance, he would have thought.

He had rather expected her to jump at his offer.

'As long as — ' She gave a deep sigh. Then hurriedly, 'Yes, I would like to. I will.'

She was terrified he was just amusing himself. She could not bear her love not to be taken seriously. She knew she was incapable of enjoying a simple affair. She was congenitally made for unhappiness, incapable of enjoying the passing moment. She saw herself quite plainly, and despaired. She was deeply, hopelessly, romantically, in love with Tom and could see no happy ending for herself. She was already thinking of the ending when there had as yet been no beginning.

'I'm sorry,' she said.

Tom could hardly be excited by her response, but supposed it was a shock. There was only a day's notice.

'We can meet here. I can bring the car up. What time?'

'I've got permission to leave early. The coach is going at five.'

'Okay. Five then.'

He thought she might change her mind. But as they got up and walked towards the gateway into the street, she caught him suddenly and flung her arms around him and kissed him.

'I'm sorry! — I'm sorry I'm like I am!'

It would have been funny if she wasn't so obviously distressed. He held her closely and said gently, 'It's for pleasure, my darling. To make us happy, not to get upset about.'

The endearment came without thought; he really meant it, seeing her terrible vulnerability. If anyone needed someone to look after her, it was Camilla. He was so unused to being needed as a protector that all his chivalrous instincts arose from long slumber and astonished him by their emotional strength. Standing in the middle of the path in front of the interested middle-aged ladies, he stroked Camilla's untidy bush of hair and said, 'I won't let you down, I promise. I really mean it, not just a one-night stand.'

He was deeply touched, responding to her need, and left her with a genuine feeling of commitment. The prospect of the weekend was now an excitement that would not leave his thoughts, and he found the evening with Jo hard to sustain, convinced she would detect the difference in him. He watched television, trying to concentrate on what he was seeing. But Jo was more concerned with Mr Baker than herself: 'If all schools were like mine, he wouldn't need his rotten Education bill!'

It was half-joke, half a fierce pride in her work, but Tom was so immersed in 'Question Time' he did not hear her.

★   ★   ★

Camilla realised that she had never been in love at all with Jake, her only past lover. What she had felt for him was a mere brushing of grateful affection compared with the passion that moved her for Tom. Her feelings for Tom frightened her. But she could not believe any happiness could emanate from the friendship because she could not see him ever leaving Jo. She had wrestled with the idea of not seeing him any more, the course her nature dictated, but could not bear to forego the wild joy that merely setting eyes on him provoked. If only she had a flat of her own where they could go it might have been workable . . . she cursed herself for not shaking herself free of her aunt. She could have afforded a flat a few years ago, but now the prices were impossible. Every decision she had ever taken in her life had been wrong! She saw herself as doomed, even when her quaking nerve-ends rejoiced in Tom's touch and his kisses turned her intended coolness to mere myth.

It was just as well the prospect of sleeping with him was sprung at the last moment, as she did not know how she could have got through more than the one day of anticipation. Companions in the office thought she was nervous about the concert; the office junior suggested she had a temperature — 'Are you sure you're well? You look feverish to me. There's this bug going round, you know.' 'Yes, I might have a bug.' Camilla found this both comforting and amusing. She had a bug all right. If only she could laugh with joy and confidence! Another of the typists was in love with a married man and hellbent on weaning him from his wife. Her determination fuelled the relationship; she rejoiced in every small victory, was obsessed by — thoroughly enjoyed — every lie and deception and hasty snatched coupling. She was aflame with physical, fighting love and happier than she had ever been when complacently married to a reasonably nice man in computers. Why, wondered Camilla, did she have none of this splendid spirit? Thinking of Jo, her rival, decimated her. It was fatal to think of Jo. She put Jo right out of her mind.

She dressed in her long black skirt and white blouse, the choir uniform, and went to meet Tom in the churchyard. He was already there, sitting on the bench, his long legs stretched out across the path. He looked very relaxed, face up towards the afternoon sun, hands in pockets. At the sight of him her nerves lurched and hammered in their absurd fashion. She stood like an idiot.

'Camilla!' Tom leapt to his feet, his face springing to life. Even in her confused state, Camilla could not mistake that he was pleased to see her. He put his arm round her and gave her a little hug.

'You're early too — good! I had a devil of a job parking the car — it's not very close, I'm afraid.'

They hurried through the swarming streets to where the smart Porsche was unclamped, unticketed, waiting to spirit them into what she now saw as paradise ahead.

During the fast run up the motorway the ridiculous euphoria steadied, replaced by a warm confidence that Camilla could never remember feeling before. She sat beside Tom wondering at her happiness, this rare condition that other people seemed to attain so easily, and she so rarely. It was worth cherishing while it was around. Showers of rain over the Newmarket bypass did not dampen her spirits and the fading of the evening into irridescent spray from hissing tyres made a soothing contribution to her mood; nothing was ugly. They approached Ely with perfect timing, coming to the great West front of the cathedral in a procession of cars unloading.

'If we go on past, there's an archway through the wall, down on the right. They said go through there.'

Tom obeyed Camilla's instructions. Through the archway a road curved back to the cathedral, whose walls, like the hulk of a great ship, reared up before them. Uneven parkland, dotted with heavy-headed old trees, sloped away into the milky film of the wet distance. The grass after the shower was near to steaming, giving off rich odours of ancient humus and the returning sunshine, late and darkly gold, slashed long fingers down amongst the leaves. Tom touched the button to let down the windows, and the rich, fresh smell of the wet earth flooded into the car. With it came a thrush's evening rhapsody from the closest tree, pouring into the evening. They sat listening.

'Who wants Berlioz?' Camilla murmured.

Tom did not move. It was perfect. A passing moment — another car drew up behind them and people got out, laughing and talking.

Camilla gave Tom his ticket.

'Shall I meet you here afterwards? There

133

will probably be an awful crush inside.'

'Very well.'

They went inside, Camilla to her place in the choir tiers and Tom to a seat in the aisle. The whole of Cambridgeshire seemed to be gathering around them, the performers taking up nearly as much room as the audience. There was much meeting up, waving from cramped seats and embracing, the great nave echoing to the crowd. Builders' scaffolding obscured a good part of the roof, the fan vaulting mostly hidden (cathedrals seemed always thus now). Tom knew that old roofs needed extra insurance cover for Berlioz. The four brass bands were hidden in the clerestory and somewhere a second conductor was lurking, to convey cues to musicians who could not see their leader. Excess was not necessarily an assurance of triumph, but an air of anticipation rippled round the packed nave as the requiem was ready to start.

For Tom there was more to it than music, but for now the music would do.

*　*　*

Camilla, singing in her choir, could not hear her own voice even though it was at full pitch proclaiming the glory of God. It was a

134

magnificent prelude to adultery, the whole cathedral apparently in tune with her own passion. The sea of sound stunned her senses. She saw the dim aisle before her with the fading pink flowers of a thousand faces upturned, transfixed. One was Tom. She had supposed the golden aura with which her feelings bathed him would have marked him in the sea before her like a navigational fix, but there was no sign. Berlioz was all, the old bombast hammering nuances into pulp. Divine noise! As her lungs blasted forth, she did not know whether she was singing for God or for lust, adoration or copulation. Tears splashed on to her music book. The woman standing next to her, who managed a delicatessen in the city, gave her a curious glance.

Tom's emotions were not unsimilar. As the requiem drew to its end he saw that Berlioz, having given the initial thrust, could help no more. His grand themes were dying in a chorus of amens to soft orchestral arpeggios, the brass bands having packed their instruments many bars before. Tom had rather thought the work would finish at full blast, getting its money's-worth from the expensive cast, but its sweet fading left him without the uplift to face his next move. He sat back as the applause, tentative at first, rose into a thunderous crescendo. The orchestration of the rest of the weekend was now up to him. The blank sheet of manuscript paper was at hand, to write on it whatever he chose.

Leaving the cathedral by its tradesmen's entrance and filling his lungs with the damp loamy air fortunately expunged these fanciful notions, and it was with a quite normal sense of excitement and daring that he unlocked the car and waited for Camilla. She was very quick, mere footsteps behind him, apparently still on a high from her experience, her cheeks bright pink, eyes glowing.

'I've never known anything like it! It was amazing! That sound — and singing full blast into it without hearing your own voice! God knows what it was like for you — did you enjoy it? Did it work?'

'It was great — yes, it was amazing, you're right.'

'Overkill, perhaps.'

'No.'

'We all enjoyed it, at least.'

It was only just going dark, streaks of dying crimson on the horizon staining the undersides of large clouds. The flat fields full of growing corn were a mere plate to support the magnificent sky. As they drove south God orchestrated the sunset for them in tune to the glory of the requiem — an andante of pigeon-grey flushing with pink and swelling into a crescendo of riotous crimson before the dark finale — all completely in tune with their mood. Cloud nine. 'Red at night, shepherd's delight' . . . and I am the shepherd, Tom thought. He could never remember being on such a high, even with Jo.

They came into a deserted Newmarket, and checked into a new anonymous sort of hotel — Tom had chosen it as suitable in his dubious mood earlier, but now wished fervently he had gone for some ancient, ivy-covered pile with five stars to suit the extravagant mood that had come upon them both — something Berliozian, with Gothic towers and fawning flunkies. It was hopeless to think of the mundane business of eating — 'I'm not hungry!' Camilla echoed his own urge and they tumbled into their room and into each other's arms almost before the automatic lock had clicked behind them.

Camilla's body needed no five-star setting, the way it worked out. It was glorious between the serviceable polyester sheets of Trusthouse Forte, ardent as he could not remember Jo for years. The whole experience was not one jot how he had imagined it would be. He had feared embarrassment, fumbling, failure even. But it was inspired. Camilla, after all, knew the mechanics of sex.

But its motivation was something different altogether, and she gave herself completely to Tom, without stopping for self-analysis. The success of their coupling was hosannas all the way, triumphant.

Afterwards they lay in a dream. From start to finish the night had been flawless. Camilla thought she was on the verge of insanity, the shock of pure happiness almost more than she could bear, having had no practice.

In the morning they lay naked, laughing and playing. Camilla's body was too thin for beauty, her breasts scarcely formed, her buttocks taut and slender, but her newfound ecstasy gave her the glow of a Rubens courtesan, it seemed to Tom. He was enchanted with her, loving her sinews and finely-chiselled clavicles, her un-equivocal jaw and arched ribcage. Where Jo was all hummocks, Camilla was angles and corners, brittle and fine. While he was loving Camilla, he felt a boundless tenderness for Jo. His abundance of love seemed more than plenty for them both. He was astounded by his good fortune. After all, Jo at her conference was doing exactly what she wanted to do, as he was with Camilla in his arms. No one was denying the other

Camilla, her defences spiked, was now natural and vivacious and actually quite funny, laughing at herself. They had the rest of the day to enjoy, and drove out to Norwich, and on to the coast where, in the softness and privacy of a sand dune on the Norfolk coast, they made love again. This time it was a quite different mood, *tranquillo* rather than *maestoso*. The sun shone thinly through a gauzy, washed-out sky, tenderly on them, not strong and glaring, and the wind was the softest of zephyrs, caressing the stiff reeds over their heads, smooth and untroubled across the sea. The beach was empty in both directions, curving like a melon slice under the huge canopy of the sky; only some gulls mewed far out at sea like the echoes of departed souls.

'It's not like England here,' Camilla said. 'So empty. I could live up here. So peaceful.'

It was a good idea, Tom thought. Not too far away, the way he drove: a flint cottage by the sea, a pram in the front garden and infant catsuits blowing on the line . . . he laughed.

'Why are you laughing?'

'I'm happy,' he said.

He knew it was going to work, and the idea of it filled him with satisfaction.

★   ★   ★

Jo was so totally occupied with her summer term and plans for the barge trip, not to mention sports day, reports, and a problem with a leaking demountable classroom, that she did not notice Tom's more frequent absences, late nights and his new cheerfulness. Tom was very careful not to be too happy but the condition of loving and being loved by two women at once was pretty good, and he couldn't help whistling at times and smiling idiotically into space during his leisure moments.

Jo assumed he had come to terms with her refusal to have a child and was accepting the situation. He was no longer moody and bad-tempered: the assumption followed and she did not want to talk about it any more. She did notice that he was more loving but was more relieved than curious. His work was going well and so was hers, and life seemed to her wholly satisfactory on all fronts.

Tom met Camilla nearly every day for lunch, but found very little opportunity to take her to bed again. This romantic frustration helped to fuel the affair. They were like teenage lovers, finding great difficulty in behaving with propriety in their usual trysting-place, the churchyard. They sat bathed in June sunshine under the warm stone walls, sharing their sandwiches. Their conversation was unremarkable, bliss complete. Camilla agreed to go away with Tom during the week that Jo was away on her barge trip, and they had the date to look forward to, the week to plan for. Tom decided he would tell her about his plans during that time, and, all being well, they might even start looking for a suitable cottage.

When Jo apologised for leaving him to his own devices for a week, he told her it didn't matter, he would go climbing in Scotland.

'We can go somewhere when I come back,' Jo said. 'I'll probably need a rest. Somewhere hot and lazy, what do you think?'

She dreamed of a Mediterranean beach, but knew she wouldn't get it. Tom hated beaches, and doing nothing.

'Okay,' he said vaguely. 'Yes, great.'

He could take a fortnight, a week with Camilla and a week with Jo. His mind soared; he was filled with love.

# 5

Jo finalised the arrangements for chartering *Adeline*. She decided on four days — three nights on board — as sufficient for nine-year-olds and drew up her list of children. Over thirty had applied to come; the trip would have to be repeated, but this would be no problem. The first would be the pilot, and she chose her children with care, taking consideration of friendships, eschewing favouritism (although she included Daniel Weston) and equalising the sexes. Stevie would accompany them, also Penny Curtis, her youngest and newest teacher, a sporty girl who usefully sailed a Laser and knew the drill. Nick was bringing a mate, a young cousin called Norm, so they would be sufficiently crewed, a ratio of adults to children of nearly one to two. Grott would have no grounds to disapprove. She drew up the sailing programme with Nick, including alternatives for bad weather, marking comfortable anchorages and convenient places to go ashore, the occasional availability of chips and ice-cream and the phone numbers of doctors on the route. Her keenest interest was in the list of the natural phenomena she had drawn up to be examined at sea or on the shore, but no one could accuse her of not taking Grottlike precautions for all available contingencies. In fact she felt his auntyish image prompting many of her actions, and was exasperated by it. He seemed to be making no attempt to apply for any headships.

'It's yours he wants,' Ros said darkly, when Jo mentioned it.

'Whatever makes him thinks I'm giving up?'

'He thinks you're bound to leave soon to have a baby. And once he's got a foot in . . . '

'Tell him Tom's stopped his hankering, so I'm set for life — that'll upset him! The sooner he knows the better.'

'Why, is it true?'

'Yes. Absolutely. Not a murmur for the last couple of months. And he's happy as a sandboy.'

'Whatever's made him change his mind?'

'I've no idea. Me saying I never would, finally, I suppose.'

'Did you?'

'Yes.'

'What if he'd said he'd leave you?'

'It did cross my mind. I don't know. I think I'd still have held out. But he didn't, and he's

143

altogether nicer now we don't argue about it any more — he's accepted it.'

'I'm amazed!'

Once or twice in the past Tom, after a few drinks, had asked Ros if she thought Jo would ever change her mind. Ros had noted the intense desire behind his questioning and had actually thought that the apparently perfect marriage was in considerable danger. It now passed through her mind that that could still be the case, but Jo was so wrapped up in her work she didn't notice. However Ros was not one to stir, and kept her surprise flippant, and changed the subject.

Jo was making out menus for the four days and estimating the quantities of food she would have to buy. The cost per head had been fixed when the invitations had been framed; now she had to work it out according to income. There was also the list of essential items for each child to bring, find out if *Adeline* was supplied with enough pillows, what about life-jackets . . . All this on top of the extra work end of term entailed. No wonder, Ros thought, Jo didn't bother to enquire into the rather unexpected turn her marriage had taken; there just wasn't room in her time-table.

When Tom packed for his climbing trip to Scotland Jo didn't notice that his rucksack was joined by a discreet suitcase full of clothes more suited to hotels than sleeping out, didn't really notice how buoyant were his spirits and kindly his attitude to all she was doing. He went to the supermarket with her to help her transport her shopping, bought a couple of gas-lanterns for *Adeline* to supplement Nick's picturesque but not very adequate oil-lights — her electrics still being liable to failure without notice — and a bottle of gin for captain's stores. He even dealt with Mrs Tranter's attempt to provide Kevin with his own food hamper — sternly, on the telephone.

'You'd make a wonderful headmaster,' Jo said admiringly when he put the receiver down.

'That must be the most fulsome compliment you've ever paid me.'

Jo went and put her arms round him. 'You are a sweetie. Will you miss me next week?'

Tom, to her surprise, hugged her in return and gave her an uncommonly affectionate kiss.

'No,' he said.

She laughed.

'I do love you, Tom.'

She did not see the look that came into his face as she said this, her own face being buried in his pullover. It was compounded of guilt, exasperation and tenderness. If his arrangement with Camilla ever came off and he set up another home, Tom knew that he was going to have to tell Jo. Some men might be able to keep such a double life a secret, but he did not fancy such a complicated deceit. He didn't fancy telling her either. His plans were not wholly delicious, after all.

He put the idea aside, and suggested they go out for a meal.

'You don't want to be an exhausted wreck before you start this barge lark.'

But she thrived on hard work. Being tired did not make her snappy and irritable, merely a mite slower and quieter. Nicer, said Tom.

They went out for a meal. Jo was sailing on the tide at midday the next day, by which time Tom knew he would be speeding north up the motorway with Camilla at his side. He should have felt a complete heel, but he felt more self-confident and loving than he could ever remember. He had chicken with cashew nuts, and they ordered a bottle of Muscadet. He always had chicken and cashew nuts. The restaurant was pink and characterless and not far from home, and Tom preferred it to more exotic sites further away. They went there often and the Chinese waiters knew them and which table they liked and it was very boring but exactly how Tom liked it. Jo would have preferred more glamour and exotic French cooking, more up-market ambience and menus without the dishes being numbered, but she knew better than to forestall Tom in his curious preferences. She also would have chosen a restaurant where they were unlikely to meet any of her parents. When Ann Forrester came in with her cold-faced solicitor husband Jo had drunk three-quarters of the Muscadet and was in no mood for technical chat, but Mrs Forrester came pointedly across to their table.

'All set to go, Mrs Monk? Rather you than me — such a responsibility! I do admire your energy!'

She was so utterly crass and ill-meaning that Jo could not summon enough of her famous energy to think of a reply. The child Forrester's name had been conspicuous by its absence from the applications to sail, no doubt nobbled by Grott.

Jo could think of no parent she disliked more than Mrs Forrester. She was ungainly and ferret-faced, nothing like the majority of her mothers who seemed no more than artless schoolchildren themselves, hung around with smaller infants than the ones they had come to collect, and bags of shopping and dogs on leads. Mrs Forrester collected her children in a car and gave no lifts to their friends. She campaigned sternly against dogs' faeces on the playing-field. Now, as she lingered, her eyes raked in every detail of what they were eating and drinking, and moved reflectively, almost insolently, over Tom.

'I understand the skipper you're using is an old friend of yours? I couldn't find him amongst the charter skippers recommended by the Country Council.'

'Excuse me, Mrs Forrester, but my wife is not on duty at the moment. We are enjoying a conversation on the development of fugue in early church music, and would like to continue it.'

Tom gave her a hard, hostile stare, and saw her expression harden into equal hostility. She was too thick-skinned to be embarrassed, but moved on without another word.

Jo giggled.

'What's fugue?'

'It's a device for getting rid of unwanted meddlers.'

'It worked a treat. I've told you how awful she is. Now you'll believe me.'

'Yes. She doesn't like you, does she?'

Jo wasn't used to being disliked.

'I've never done anything to make her dislike me, not that I can think of.'

'You have.'

'What?'

'Made a colossal success of your school, made yourself loved and admired. I should say she's very jealous, being all the things you're not.'

Jo giggled again. 'About this fugue then — ?'

In spite of the interruption, it was as amicable an evening as they had enjoyed for a long time, and when they went to bed they made love with great enjoyment. Tom failed to feel a cheat and a cad, but felt rich and magnanimous and lucky beyond belief.

★   ★   ★

Jo had arranged to meet the children on the quay beside *Adeline* an hour before high water. Most of the parents had come to see them off, the pushy Tranters along with the silent Liz Weston. Jo noticed that parting from Daniel was agony for Liz, and kicked herself that she hadn't asked her to come along too. It would have been awkward, but not impossible. On the other hand the boy would benefit from a few days away from the understandably claustrophobic love of his mother. Since his father's death Daniel had become an anxious child. Jo had a few words with Liz.

149

'I'll get him to ring you when we go ashore. You'll miss him terribly, but it's only four days!'

'I'm a dreadful fool.'

'No. It's natural.'

At least, if she fussed, it wasn't obvious. She was a reserved woman, and bottled up her feelings, which was why she couldn't come to terms with her husband's death. She needed to forget Daniel and go out on the town, but it was not in her nature. Jo reminded herself to try and do more to find her some interests after the holiday.

The children trooped on board, chattering and excited, and went below to find their berths. The parents hung about on the quay, waiting to watch the barge sail, but when Jo said it wouldn't be for some time, most of them dispersed. The children had to have a lecture first from Nick about safety regulations and how to behave on board a boat, and their kit had to be tidily stored away. Stevie had arrived in his normal leather gear, with a minimum of luggage — one towel and a sleeping-bag as far as Joe could make out — but Penny Curtis was transformed from neat schoolteacher to unmistakable mate, in navy dungarees and yellow wellies, her hair tied back under a bobble hat. She was a hearty girl and Jo found too much of her irritating; she made Jo feel old. But her enthusiasm was ideal for the sailing trip; she was in her element and took on a new dimension once on board, which Jo noticed with satisfaction. People doing what they were best at naturally appeared at their best, and Jo knew she had made a good decision in inviting her. What with Nick making an obvious hit with the children in the saloon, and cousin Norm organising the galley, Jo began to think she might even have something of a holiday week herself.

Jo liked sailing. She was always sorry that Tom wouldn't swap his allegiance to mountains for the sea, but he couldn't be bothered with what he called 'the messing about' involved with keeping a boat. They lived on a cruising coast par excellence, as far from mountains as any place in Britain — it would have been so much more convenient to have a handy sport which they could do together. But Tom was not to be side-tracked, and Jo had given up her sailing. But when a sail blossomed above her head once more and she heard the murmur of the tide against a gently-heeling topside the old pleasure seized her. She remembered Ann Forrester's remark at the governors' meeting about her good holiday ideas — 'usually ideas in which she herself has an interest'

— and smiled. The old bat!

*Adeline* murmured her way towards the sea, the prevailing south-westerly fair in her huge new mainsail. The weather was kind, the forecast good. On the far end of the seawall beyond the two a single figure stood watching them go: Liz Weston. Jo, in her present content, felt a pang of compassion, also a touch of annoyance. Daniel needed to cut loose, growing old before his time, caring too much for others. Jo wanted him to be naughty, selfish, insolent even, in the Kevin Tranter style — it would herald his recuperation from his father's death. She would never be able to explain this to Liz.

'But I'm on holiday . . . ' Pointless to worry about what she could not do. She sat with her back against the hatch, watching Nick let the children take turns on the wheel. The children were, for once, totally immersed in this new experience, not a single one betraying that terrible fashionable ennui of being wise to everything that life had to offer. Stevie had found a new mate in the admirable Norm. They made a strange pair, discussing motorbikes with the children climbing around them, the one so black and spiky, the other bulky and rustic-looking with his slow smile and the sun-bleached thatch of hair that was so completely innocent of the craft that inspired Stevie's. Penny was teaching a small group how to tie a bowline — 'Make sure that the rabbit-hole is in front of the tree . . . the rabbit comes out of the hole, like this, round the tree and back in again . . . ' The water was as nearly blue as it could manage in these shoal and mud-broached waters, smooth and inviting to its hazy horizon where white holiday sails bobbed companionably.

Jo leaned back and felt the July sun warming her breast through her T-shirt. She was completely relaxed, consciously enjoying this rare feeling. The steady motion of the barge, the children's voices, happy and excited, mingling with the creeking of old timbers and the hissing of water under the leeboard, made up simple bliss. For a moment life was suspended, responsibilities forgotten. She could see Daniel's anxious eyes on the compass, trying to work out what the needle was doing as Nick made him alter course; she could see a little girl called Bow who cared intensely (and unnaturally, considering her age) for her appearance recoiling in horror as Norm suggested she tried flaking down one of the wet and muddy mooring warps — 'Don't want the boys to do all the deck work, do we? We'll make them cook the supper, how about that?' Shrieks of delight, theatrical groans, and Bow got the first flick of mud on her white jeans as she grasped the rope. 'Like this,' said Norm.

*Adeline* slipped down the river and Jo held her face up to the sun.

★ ★ ★

Meanwhile Tom and Camilla sped up the M1 in the Porsche, headed for the Cairngorms. Tom had decided on a leisurely journey, and a night's stop somewhere in the Dales. He knew the Dales well, and took the road up Wharfedale. There were any number of places they could stay the night, and he picked a Bed and Breakfast where he had stayed before, a very old, well-appointed cottage lying back up a track from the road. The landlady was quiet and efficient, not given to chat, respecting privacy, and the rooms were graciously furnished. It was a matter of luck as to whether it turned out happily but, in the mood they were in, a doss-house in the East End would have flourished a star or two.

As it happened Tom's favourite room was free. Two quiet, elderly walkers were the only other guests. Mrs Haythorn showed them up the stairs, asked about breakfast, and left them alone. Camilla went to the window and leaned her arms on the wide sill, looking out on a garden, stone walls, and the narrow lane down to the road, filled now with a small herd of cows coming up from the fields opposite. The sky seemed filled with the great dun whale-back of the hill across the valley. Not here the glamorous sunsets of East Anglia, but a homely darkening of the narrow sky caught between high fell and low lintel. Camilla was wrenched by its tranquility. The cows moved below her like great snails, unchivvied, and a gentle lowing from the farmyard higher up was echoed by the far-distant bleating of sheep on the evening hillside, a sad and lonely, familiar cry from her Scottish childhood. Tom joined her, looking down on the cows.

'Commuters,' he said. 'Morning and evening.'

'So unhurried!'

'All the time in the world! So've we now — a whole week.' After snatched dinner-hours it seemed amazing largesse.

'We've only just started, yet it's perfect already.'

'More perfect still — there's a pub a mile or two up that lane opposite where they do smashing dinners.'

They went out and down the lane. The hill behind them was flushed gold with the light of the dying sun, the one before them purple

155

dark, in silhouette. They crossed the road that came from London, quiet and empty in the dusk, and took a lane that led between flowering hedges and wide water-meadows, following a river up a valley. A chill came from the damp grass, and the smell of crushed stalks and wild peppermint where the cows had been grazing drifted from the river bank. The valley was narrow and dark, no lights showing save the first star above the high ridge ahead.

'I don't believe there's food up here,' Camilla said. 'You're making it up.'

'Want to bet?'

'No. I want to eat.'

'I'm honing your appetite. There's a pub, I promise, and a church too, if you want to pray.'

'There's nothing to pray for, save thanks. I've got everything I want.'

Tom had too, save for a pang towards Jo, deceived. He was not a natural adulterer, and it surprised him how easily it came.

The valley narrowed rapidly and the river closed in to the road and fell noisily down beside it. The pub was squashed between the lane and the steep hill it backed on to. Its lights splashed in the river below and showed a bridge crossing and the outline of an ancient church on the other side, crouching among dark yews.

'You can take your choice — flesh or the soul. Left or right. Myself, I'm for the pub.'

Tom pushed open the door.

The pub was ancient and homely, the food good, the natives friendly. When they had finished they walked back down the lane, hand in hand, and Camilla said, 'I can't think why I've stayed in London so long. You only realise how awful it is when you come to somewhere like this.'

'But you didn't like Scotland.'

'I was leaving my family more than Scotland. I'm a country person really — I've never been happy in London. Not like I could be happy in a place like this, if there was a living here.'

'It would be cheap enough to live up here, I should imagine. And the property must be a quarter of the price.'

Tom was anxious not to move too fast, yet Camilla was adept at giving him openings. 'Wouldn't you be bored?'

'Not if I had my own place. Never. An old cottage and a bit of garden, and books to read, and records to play. It would be paradise! How could you ever be bored?'

'I know a lot of people who would.'

'Would you?'

'I'd need my work. I like my work. But if I

157

had that, no, I'd be happy in a place like this. Great to have the walking so close. You could go every weekend.'

Not many of the publishers he worked for stemmed from the Yorkshire Dales. There would have to be a lot of to-ing and fro-ing. The Porsche would come into its own. Three hours from London without hold-ups? To find Camilla in a cottage, waiting for him . . . His mind kept running ahead, a terrier excited by every scent thrown up.

They went back to their B and B, refused an invitation to watch the television and have a pot of tea, and went up to their room.

Camilla said, 'This bedroom — it could be mine, how I would have it.'

'A double bed?'

'For visitors!'

The bed was covered by a faded quilt and the sheets smelled of sun and wind and were made of cotton, not slippery nylon. They had been waiting for them all day, Camilla thought as she turned to Tom. She cried for joy, so practised at crying but never knowing until now that it could be used for sheer bliss as readily as for the deepest depression.

'Tom, oh Tom!' she wept.

He kissed her tears and stroked her thick hair.

'Don't cry! Don't cry!'

What was he doing to her, he wondered?

In the morning Camilla lay and studied every detail of her surroundings, because the day was perfect and she was going to remember it for ever: every tremulous pattern of the pale wallpaper, every hairline crack in the severely whitewashed ceiling, the texture of the blankets, the smell of the garden flowers from the open window. She was happy now as she never had been and never expected to be again, and everything had to be computerised in her brain for later recall: When Tom is gone, Camilla thought, having no optimism, when I am back in my curdled room in Covent Garden, I will remember the ceiling of this room and its thick, thick walls binding us round and this lovely bed smelling of fields. And Tom. And Tom. And Tom. When he loved her again she cried some more.

'You're a very weepy woman,' Tom said, smiling.

'Yes, I'm sorry. I can't help it.'

'It's so nice here. Shall we stay another night?'

'Yes.'

'And sleep in this bed again. And climb the hill opposite and have lunch in the next valley. And walk back again, and have supper in the same pub.'

'Yes.'

The cows went down the lane again and Tom and Camilla had their breakfast with the two quiet walkers. They had eggs and bacon and sausages and mushrooms and fried bread, toast and marmalade and tea, which seemed a satisfactory start to a walking day. The day was fine, with hazy sunshine and scarcely any wind, and the forecast good.

They crossed the river and set off along the path which led steeply up the side of the hill. Camilla was not a practised walker like Tom, but was strong and fit, and knew enough to shorten her stride the steeper it got. If she followed Tom, it seemed easier.

'Yorkshire's great,' said Tom as they came on to the brow. 'It's not high anywhere, so you're soon up . . . it's for the elderly, and people on their first day of hols.'

They strode steadily over the sheep-grazed summit until the view into the next dale fell away below them. 'We'll keep high,' Tom said, 'and home in to the pub at the top of the valley.'

It was almost urban, to Tom's way of thinking, for he usually kept far from tracks and pubs, but excellently suited to the occasion. The walking was easy and Camilla strode over the yellow grass as she strode down Cheapside, looking in fact far more at

160

home. The day produced huge pillowy clouds which chased shadows across the valley and turned the far horizons to smoky purple in their passing. The hills were all colours, changing as they receded, ridge behind ridge, in every direction — a total abandonment to space and freedom. They lunched in the small pub amongst a cluster of stone cottages at the top of the valley, then climbed over the ridge to the head of the valley they had walked up the evening before. Camilla was tired now, but tried not to show it, marvelling at Tom's ease over the rough ground as they dropped down. He had to keep waiting for her. Her shins ached.

'Are are sure this is the right valley, where the pub is?'

'Yes.'

'If it isn't, you'll have to carry me.'

'I promise!'

He was right, and a large supper was forthcoming only a mile farther on, and Camilla's strength was restored sufficiently for her to walk the rest of the way to their B and B cottage. They came back into the village just as it was going dusk, earlier than the night before. The cows were crossing the bridge over the river ahead of them, and they waited while the cowman came past, and his dog stopped for a quick drink on the bank.

161

'Look,' Camilla said as they waited.

Beside the bridge a short track ran up to a cottage that stood on its own, back to the hill, on the edge of the village. A sign stood by its garden gate, proclaiming it for sale.

'There's my cottage.'

The windows were blank and uncurtained and the garden overgrown.

'It's empty. Let's look in the windows.'

Camilla set off up the track and Tom followed. It was nothing he had arranged yet, watching Camilla unfasten the gate and walk up to the front door, Tom felt that some unseen hand was taking a part in his affairs. Camilla standing in that unkempt garden, looking back at him and smiling, was part of his daft dream — Camilla his kept woman, bearing his child, made happy by domesticity and country life, roses round the door: all in the mind, it was now staring him in the face. Last night he had been voicing his opinion that property might be cheap in the area; now the property stood before him and Camilla was saying, 'Look, it's been empty for ages. No one wants it. I bet it would be quite cheap.'

'Why, do you like it?'

'It's heavenly. My dream cottage.'

She was peering in the front windows, hands cupped to stop the reflection.

162

'Look, look at this sweet room.'

The ceiling was low, held by two blackened beams, the floor stone flagged. No attempt had been made to modernise it, the fireplace filled by the traditional range and oven. A wooden staircase went up out of one corner, and there was still furniture in it: a scrubbed wooden table and chairs, and a sagging armchair with squashed cushions.

'Strange, it looks as if it's just waiting for someone to come back,' Camilla said.

She walked round the back, picking her way past a rampant patch of parsley and the trailers from a huge rambling rose sporting cream, sweet-scented flowers.

Camilla sniffed one. 'Alberic Barbier,' she said.

Tom's jaw dropped. He could not trust his voice. He followed.

'A perfect kitchen, facing east. This is east, isn't it? The morning sun — and look, the door opens on to these flags. Breakfast outside if the weather's right. Just how I would have chosen.'

There were only two rooms downstairs and — presumably — up. The roof was slated, with a dormer window facing over the river. The walls were of stone, as thick as those where they were staying.

'No central heating,' Tom said, 'no bath, no

damp course, no insulation.' His voice sounded strange, even to himself.

'Life is not all about central heating,' Camilla said.

Her face was smoothed out, madonna-like. Her eyes shone and her cheeks were creamy-pink. She was the very vision of woman ripe for motherhood, like a nineteen-thirties magazine cover, with Ovaltine advertised on the inside.

'If this were mine,' she said, 'I wouldn't ever want anything else ever.'

Very carefully, Tom said nothing at all. His senses cried out to tell her it was hers, he would make her dream come true, he would set her up. She could have his children and live happily ever after. But it was as if he sensed a trap: the bait was so perfect, it was everything he had planned. He could not bring himself to make the commitment. Not yet. He had never been impulsive; he lacked true generosity; he was too selfish. He saw the opportunity before him, Camilla radiant with her day and her cottage standing in the last fading golden light that still reached over the fells, picking a rose called Alberic Barbier to fix in her buttonhole . . . the rose was too much.

When they drove on in the morning, he stopped in the next town to enquire in the house agent's about the cottage. It was indeed very cheap and the agent said they were prepared to let it for the time being. He told Camilla his mother was looking for something like it, but to himself he decided that by the end of the week — on the way home — he would very likely decide to buy it for Camilla. He could afford it. He would give himself the five days left to make up his mind.

As they got back in the car and headed over the dale towards Carlisle, he felt extraordinarily optimistic.

# 6

Daniel watched Norm dropping an old tin bucket over the side on the end of a rope, filling it with water and pulling it back on board to wash the mud off the deck.

'Can I do that?'

'Naw. You can use the brush, if you like.'

Norm, not used to talking much, remembered he was now part of a teaching set-up.

'S'not as easy as you think. The tide takes the bucket, like, gives it a pull. Really strong. Don't want you to lose the bucket now, do we? Skipper'd be mad.'

The way he did it, with a flick of the wrist, fascinated Daniel. Kevin Tranter came over, attracted by something forbidden.

'Bet I could do it.'

'You're not getting the chance, mate.'

Norm, who looked slow, was sharp at picking up which of the kids were worth their salt. Kevin had no concentration and could not be relied upon to do anything for longer than five minutes. He would sneak out of all the boring jobs but opt quickly for the privileges. But Daniel with his dogged interest in how things worked would tussle for hours to master a difficulty. He had learned all the useful knots, how to splice a rope, steer a course, light a pressure lamp, work a leeboard. He never complained, or took the last chocolate biscuit.

'Your dad'd be proud of you,' Nick said to him early on, when he had put the barge about without advice, filling the backed sail to a nicety without laying off too far on the new tack.

'I haven't got one.'

'Oh. Bad luck, boy.'

But Daniel was happier than he'd ever been since his father's death. Jo saw the change in him and knew, if only for this child alone, her trip was worth all her trouble. He cleaned the deck meticulously as Norm threw down the water, but Kevin, seeing no glamour in scrubbing, sauntered away to find something more worthy of his talents.

They were going ashore and Nick was letting the tender down off its davits. The barge lay in deep water off a rare sandy beach where sandpipers and oyster-catchers were fishing along the waterline. A cormorant sat on a stake, preening its feathers, and along the seawall all manner of plants grew unscathed, including sea-spinach which Jo reckoned they could pick and eat for supper. If there was enough driftwood they could make a fire and sit out in the dusk . . . Jo had a hankering for past fires of her childhood, and singing camp songs to the soft explosions of sparks from resinous pine. She was always conscious of what memories her children might cherish from what she was able to lay before them, aware of her own, and the haphazard nature of what was picked up from childhood. Pictures on the walls of the classroom were important, and pictures in the mind, and smells, and friendships. It was a matter of showing possibilities, leaching out talent, opening up paths; it was never-ending, the commitment, she could not leave it alone. She had a fleeting thought for Tom in his lonely mountains, and a sigh of guilt which she knew would not stop her. She could not help herself, it had become a habit.

Scouring the seashore with her children — 'You can find cornelian here, and amber' — she was as happy as they were. Looking for things, you found more than you ever guessed at. Bow had oil on her once white jeans, but was excited about a starfish; two boys were bringing back a very dead seagull. Nick had spread out an old dinghy sail for the children to put their findings on, and shells and bones and scoured glass and whitened twigs and seaweed and golden samphire were all arriving — 'No, don't pick any flowers! We can see the sea-holly without taking it. You can draw the flower in your books and write where it was growing. Find its name in the Wildflower book.' They found a quay and the remains of an old railway line running inland, which had once taken goods from barges, and where the barges had moored up there were bits of old plates, a tin teapot half buried and an old ropework fender. When they lay in the sun on the top of the seawall there was nothing to be seen inland save miles of pasture seamed with ditches, and some cattle grazing here and there; far in the distance milky-blue woods touched the sky and the larks rose up, singing, over their heads. Some of these children did not know such places existed off the television screen.

'If you live here, miss, what do you do?'

Nick looked at Jo and laughed. They had once camped on this beach and swum naked, and ridden an old carthorse that had been grazing on the wall.

'You collect things. You make a fire and cook your tea. You walk to town if you want towny things.'

'How far is that, miss?'

'Nick will show you on his chart, where we are, and you can see where the nearest town is. You can make your own map of where we've been in the barge. We can have a competition for the best map.'

'There's something on the chart called Abraham's Bosom, miss!'

'It's a hole in a sandbank,' Nick said. 'Like a little harbour, but under water. Barges used it.'

'You can see the sandbank out towards the horizon, if you look. It's sticking up now because it's low water. At high water it's covered up but there are buoys to mark it, so that a boat doesn't hit it.'

'What happens if a boat hits it?'

'In bad weather it could wreck it. The sand is hard out there, and the waves bump a hull and break it open. That's why you can't just go anywhere, you have to read a chart and go where the water's deep.'

'I can navigate,' said Kevin.

'Good. You can navigate when we leave, and tell Nick where the good water is.'

Kevin looked worried and walked away.

'Hope there's no wildfowlers around — Stevie might get shot,' Nick said.

Jo laughed. Stevie at the water's edge on his amazing thin legs looked like a migrating exotic, crest ruffled by the breeze. The oyster-catchers ignored him, picking their way past.

'Such a strange boy! It's hard to tell how his mind works. He never says anything to us

170

at school, beyond the odd grunt or two, yet seems perfectly happy. I never asked him to stay, but . . . ' Crispin Grott, not understanding, wanted him to go. Jo, not understanding, wanted to see how things worked out.

'Perhaps he harbours a secret passion for you.'

Jo laughed.

'Like me,' Nick said.

'You had your chance years ago! But you preferred *Adeline*.'

'Well, yes. But both would have been nice.'

'When I finish work, I want a bit of relaxation. Not get down the fo'c'sle with a paintbrush, thank you. Whoever you marry will have to take on *Adeline* too.'

'A privilege.'

'Doubtful.'

Jo was amused. Nick was the brother she never had. She could not believe that he had anything but brotherly feelings for her too.

'What about this fire? Is there enough driftwood to make it worthwhile?'

'Yes, easily.'

They had lit theirs, years ago, with the help of tar off the seawall. Strange what one remembered! She went to look, moved by her carefree memories and Nick's unexpected declaration. She was reliving her past, pretending it was for the children. But they were lapping it up, proving that human nature did not change a lot, only the surface appearance. Later, in the dusk, their faces glowed in the dancing firelight and they sang eagerly the songs she remembered and taught them, not despising them in favour of pop.

'*Clop*, clop, *clop*, clop, we're *out* on the *road* again,

The *sun*'s up be*hind* us and the *day*'s just be*gun* . . . '

They made the noise of the horses' hooves by linking their fingers together and banging the heels of their hands. They thought it was wonderful.

'Orderly, tish! Orderly, tosh!

Orderly, tea this way!

Oh, who would be an orderly upon an orderly day?'

They shouted it out at the tops of their voices and the smoke spun in the offshore breeze and the stars came out.

'That's Orion with his belt. The three stars are his belt, can you see? . . . '

She could not stop, she was an idiot, a non-stop, congenital teacher. She should never have married poor Tom, who did not understand.

★　★　★

'What about this one?'

Tom slowed the car as they came to a bend. There was a house standing back up a drive with a notice out for B and B. It was surrounded by woods, and a stream could be heard falling noisily down a glen somewhere close by. Behind, high moors could be seen through gaps in the trees.

'We haven't much choice up here. This looks nice.'

Camilla wanted to keep out of the Spey valley where her family and her face were known. The by-road ran parallel, but was out of the way.

Tom pulled into the drive and shut off the engine.

'We'll go and see.'

The door was open, and someone was playing a piano. Two Labradors were lying outside in the sun and merely wagged their tails indolently at the visitors.

'Anyone around?' Tom shouted.

A boy of about six came into the hall and stared at them, then turned and shouted, 'Daddy! Someone's come!'

The piano stopped abruptly and a man came out. He was much the same age as Tom and spoke with a home counties accent as he showed them a room.

'We're not very smart yet, I'm afraid. But

173

the beds are comfortable enough. Bathroom's next door, plenty of hot water. Evening meal too, if you want it.'

The informality was attractive, the rather down-at-heel, Victorian house exuding a welcoming but take-it-or-leave-it air. Several children seemed to take visitors for granted, like the dogs. There was a smell of cooking and clatter of saucepans from the kitchen.

'Yes, great. Two more for supper please.'

They parked the car and shifted their baggage into the bedroom, where the evening sun was slanting in through the pine trees.

'We'll climb up there tomorrow,' Tom promised. 'Your home ground — you'll know the way.'

'I've never been up there in my life!'

'Time you did then. I like this place.'

It belonged to a couple who had opted out from London commuter life. Fred, the piano-player, had been an accountant in the city, and had sold a house in Chalfont St Giles to retreat from the rat-race.

'We found this place when we were on holiday, and it was for sale. It seemed to want us, somehow. We only thought about it for two days, and bought it before we went home. That was two years ago, and we haven't regretted it — wished we'd done it earlier, actually.'

He was banging an assortment of cutlery and mats down on a huge, scrubbed table.

'Betty's a teacher. She'll probably go back to it before long — the youngest's only three though. I spend most of my time getting this place straight. It was in pretty bad condition when we bought it, and there's still tons to do. Want a drink while we're waiting? Betty likes to get the kids into bed before we eat.'

The bottle of red wine he opened was presumably a remnant of the old ways — 'We don't give ourselves entirely to the simple life up here.' He grinned. They sat on ancient, rather doggy sofas in a book-lined lounge and he filled large glasses and set them down at their feet.

'I used to get through crates of this stuff — now it's more often a cup of tea . . . when you've been sawing and hammering all day, it's more what you feel like. Funny, isn't it, how far away you can get from real life when you're on that London treadmill? Makes me sweat to think of it now.'

He talked with such conviction that Tom felt envious.

'When they opened the M25 you could hear the traffic all day, all night, it never stopped. Where are they all going? Betty got paranoic about it. We both agreed on this place, we fell on it — only hesitated the two days because of giving up our livelihood. But once you've made the break — you wonder how you ever survived before.'

Tom thought, but didn't say, being a tactful man, what about Chernobyl? When you think you've escaped the modern world, it tricks you by dropping radiation not over the teeming cities but over the wilderness where people go to opt out. He knew he could not do a Fred. For all his passion for lonely places, he needed the stimulus of city life to give him direction.

Fred's wine was good. Betty, arriving damp from bathing the children, was a thin, lively woman full of nervous energy. She was still very Chalfont St Giles, but eager with love of her new estate. She wore large spectacles and her hair was pulled severely back to be practical. Her cooking was plain but substantial. They sat round the dining table like old friends, Fred pouring the wine lavishly. Camilla denied being married to Tom when the question arose, but Jo never came into the conversation at all. She did not exist. Camilla felt herself flowering in her own right as this hospitable couple accepted her as Tom's partner. Her tongue was loosened, her inhibitions forgotten; she could talk about music and books and the problems of the modern world, conversation for which their hosts had a great appetite, their days passing normally with consideration only for repairing the damp-course, getting to the cash and carry, bringing in logs, changing the sheets and similar mundane compulsions.

Another couple arrived late, when they were into the brandy, and Betty had to woozle her way upstairs to show them a room. The sun had set behind the pine woods, and the open door brought a great damp scent of peat and pineneedles. Fred stood there, breathing deeply.

'Just smell that! Isn't that worth eleven quid a night? What do you say? Better than the scent of the M25 in your garden, eh? What do you think?'

'It's great.' Tom couldn't wait to get into bed with Camilla. She was like a full-blown rhododendron, black and pink and glowing. He was a little drunk, he knew. Their bedroom smelled of wet rot and new paint, but through the open windows Fred's nectar came out of the dark woods.

'I love you! I love you!'

Camilla's arms were strong as a chimpanzee's. Loosened from her aura of despair she was an amazing girl. Tom lost himself, his cautions fled, and as he thrust into her across the quaking bed he knew he could not put off his declaration any longer. When they were both spent and she was weeping her usual drenching tears — a rhododendron in the Scottish rain — he said, 'I want you to have a baby, Camilla. My baby — our baby — will you? I will look after you both. I want it so badly!'

She looked at him as if he had gone mad.

'You said you wanted one!'

Had he got it all wrong? Was it an insult, after all, that he wanted her for what she could give him, not for herself?

She stared at him from her pillow, trembling. Tom could hear the people next door cleaning their teeth and talking to each other. They must have heard the great climactic creaking of Fred's old bed a few minutes earlier, unless they were stone deaf. The plumbing gurgled and sang.

'I love you, Camilla. I want to make you happy. Would it make you happy? It would me.'

'What would I do?'

'I'd keep you, in a cottage somewhere — the one we saw this morning, if you like. Or anywhere, you could choose.'

'And live with me?'

'Sometimes. Sometimes not. There's Jo, you see. I don't know how it would work.'

'She would leave you!'

Tom did not see why she should, given the

choice, but knew there were areas he could not fathom in women's thinking. Other men had mistresses; it had been (still was?) the accepted thing in France, and anywhere, come to that, amongst people rich enough to afford it. And his reason was not lust, but Godly procreation, surely a noble motive?

Camilla lay staring at the ceiling now, her wet dark eyes enormous with her thoughts. What they were, Tom could not tell. He could not begin to understand her tears, her fears, her introspections. He thought he was offering her something she might be glad of.

To Camilla, the offer was like a door opening into paradise. She did not dare look in, it was too overwhelming. That cottage, and Tom, and a child . . . and all she had thought of in the past as joy was Danny the dog coming back to life. It was too much to take in.

'Oh, God! oh, God!' she moaned.

Tom was worried. He did not do things with aplomb, like his father — had he blown it?

'Camilla, you're not offended?'

She thought he was mad.

'Oh, Tom, I can't believe it! Yes, yes, yes!'

He had got it right, thank God. A great surge of tenderness rose up in him, and he hugged his damp, shivering Camilla to his chest, stroking her wild hair and kissing her tears. It was wonderful to feel so protective and fatherly, it made him feel incredibly important. Independent women like Jo denied a man quite a lot — he had never appreciated it before. Camilla really needed him; he could change her deep unhappiness into pure joy with his love and care for her.

They could think about the problems later.

★  ★  ★

On the last night of the trip, *Adeline*'s anchor was let down in the mouth of her home river. She would go up on the tide in the morning, and the parents would be there to meet the children.

The three days had been a total success. The children had been marvellous, full of enthusiasm and curiosity, and Jo knew that she had given them something very valuable. The experience had brought out unexpected facets in the children's nature; they had discovered things about themselves as well as the nature of the sea and the marshes: Daniel had flowered; Bow had shown that her beautiful turnouts had been entirely the handwork of her mother — her own inclinations were careless and vanity was completely absent. Even Kevin had revealed

180

some unexpected talents: he was a confident cook, and praise for his scrambled eggs — 'I'm really good at them, miss, honest!' — had produced a sunnier and more affirmative frame of mind. Jo knew she had done well and was happily exhausted on the last evening, relaxed, and looking forward to showing the doubting Grott and snide Forrester what real teaching was all about.

The children were clearing up after supper, noisy with the washing-up, fighting over the best of the weary tea-towels. The big stew pan needed soaking.

'We can put it in a bucket of water for now,' Penny decided.

'The bucket's got those crabs in it, miss!'

'Oh. We'll have to throw them back then.'

'Not yet, miss! They're our pets!'

'You can't take them home, twits! They'll have to go back in the river.'

'Not yet though! In the morning!'

'All right. We'll have to use the deck bucket. Who'll go and fetch it?'

'Me, miss!'

'I will!'

'Daniel then, off you go.'

Jo had poured herself a large tonic and a small gin and taken another to Nick in his cuddy where he was writing his brief log.

'It's been great, Nick.'

'Yeah, they've enjoyed it, haven't they? Done 'em good, I reckon, shown 'em a bit of real life.'

'Children are very protected these days. They miss out on a lot, in some ways.'

'Namby-pambyed.'

'Yes. But once they died of rheumatic fever through walking miles to school in the pouring rain, and sitting in wet clothes all day.'

'Now they die of boredom getting it all done for them.'

'Funny, isn't it? Fifty years ago the children at home all went to school across the river. Can you imagine it, when the tide was high and running and the wind blowing in the winter? The ferryman must've been a stoic.'

'They never thought twice about it, I daresay. Children'd know about tides in those days, know the dangers.'

'Well, they've learnt a little bit this week.'

'A fraction.' Nick grinned.

They clinked glasses. Nick put his arm out, pulled Jo to him and gave her a kiss on the cheek.

'Just like old times.'

'Miss.'

Stevie stood in the doorway.

'What is it?'

'Miss Curtis said to fetch the skipper.

There's water all over the floor, coming in somewhere.'

Nick didn't look too alarmed, but they went to investigate.

'We're sinking!'

'The children were all cavorting about and Penny's backside was sticking out of the locker under the sink. Water was spurting out on to the floor from the recesses.

'Let me see.'

Nick got down beside her.

'There's a hose come loose. It's the washing-up water — '

'Jubilee clip's come off, most likely.'

Penny shuffled out to let Nick in. Her jeans were soaking wet.

'Ugh, what a pong!'

'Go and change them,' Jo said.

The children mopped up the floor with cloths, squeezing them into the stewpot that needed soaking while Nick repaired the damage.

'Put the dishes away. The tea-towels can go on the line over the fire.' Jo took over from Penny, and shooed the children out of the galley when the work was done. After supper they always worked round the big saloon table, filling up their logs of the day and mounting up their trophies. The more earnest children were already ensconced, and had to be shoved up. The table was only just big enough for the children and their projects when all were at it together.

Tonight there seemed to be more room.

'Who's missing?' Jo asked.

Only Nick and Penny were still in the galley. Norm and Steve were doing something to the engine.

'Daniel, miss. And Kevin. They went to get the bucket.'

'The bucket's there.'

'No, the deck bucket, miss.'

Jo went to call them down. The deck bucket was kept by the wheel, just aft of the hatchway. It was just going dark, and when Jo put her head out of the hatch the night air smelled fresh and soft.

'Daniel?'

There was nobody there. The bucket was gone. Jo climbed out on deck.

'Daniel!' She raised her voice. 'Daniel? Kevin?'

She climbed out and looked out along the length of the deck. It was empty. A fine sliver of a moon hung in the shrouds.

She stood there, very still.

What if . . . ?

They must be below. They saw the moon shining and the empty deck, and took the bucket and walked along the deck to the fo'c'sle hatchway, to make the most of their errand. They were not allowed on deck without life-jackets on. The life-jackets hung in a row just inside the aft hatchway. She bobbed down and counted them. There were twelve. She went back into the galley, into the saloon, quickly, quietly, and looked all through the sleeping quarters and in the loos and the sail locker and the fo'c'sle where Norm and Stevie slept. They were nowhere.

She went back on deck again. She was trembling violently and a hideous bile of sickness rose in her gorge. She went to the stern and looked over. The tide hissed against the rudder, running seaward, and specks of phosphoresence glittered at its haste. The river was wide and smooth and empty beyond, just beginning to silver under the moon. It was bland and innocent and beautiful. Jo stared. A wader croaked from the shore and, somewhere far away, a dog was barking.

Jo went below.

'Nick!'

He saw her face and came instantly.

'What is it? Oh, Jo, tell me, what's happened?'

★　★　★

Tom and Camilla sat on the rocks above Loch Einich eating Betty's healthy wholemeal sandwiches. The Cairngorms above the far side were bathed in a hazy violet light, indistinct almost to disappearance. They were high — 'Over the Munro line,' said Tom.

'What's that?'

'Three thousand feet.'

'It's heaven.'

'Give or take a few miles.'

Camilla shone and glittered and glowed like a diamond. Tom was almost afraid of being responsible for such a transformation, remembering the flinty female of their first meeting, her scratchy edges and bitter words. The world, to suit Camilla, was all sweetness, the lack of visibility caused by heat, not freezing fog, the air still save for the softest of zephyrs winging up from the still waters of the loch far below. They had climbed steadily up over heather and scratty grass, holding sweaty hands like a pair of teenagers. Tom was as excited as he remembered feeling when Jo agreed to marry him; it was not a good similarity to recall but the only one that fitted. He was too excited so far to consider what his position was likely to be when he had two wives. The future was knotty, but at the moment he regretted nothing. The world was assuredly on their side, the rocks warm in

186

the sunshine and ravens drifting in the thermals above the lake. The ridge stretched before them, imperceptibly dropping.

'Funny to think this is my home, yet I never walked up here before,' Camilla said. 'If it were clearer, I could see my family's house from this ridge.'

'Do you want to call?'

'No! Don't spoil it. We can some time. Not now.'

Tom had never been a man for families. But when he had his own, it would be different. The baby Monk, possibly conceived on a Cairngorm? . . . Camilla had put her contraception pills down Fred's lavatory.

'Will you tell Jo?'

'Yes.'

'What will she do?'

'I don't know. I think she will accept it. She's very practical.'

'You're offering me a half-share — half-share in a husband?'

'I suppose so. Will it work — for you? You ought to have thought about it a bit more — ' Before throwing the pills away, he meant.

'I'd rather share you with Jo than not have you at all.'

On the top of the mountain, in the sunshine, it all seemed perfectly practical and not very complicated. In the back of his mind

Tom doubted if it actually was, but he was sure, all parties being intelligent and no one being deceived, that any problems could be resolved. Human nature had a way of throwing a spanner in the works, but that was a risk he was taking. It was easier for him than for the two girls.

They walked down, the sun on their backs, following the ridge and its outcrops of rock, and then dropping down through the pine woods over boulders and spent timber to the bogs and river below. The walk to Loch an Eilein and round its oozy banks and paths of pine-needles to where Fred said he'd meet them in his Landrover was then a civilised ramble, meeting ladies in stout brogues with their dogs, and families in jeans. Back at home the children's voices echoed through the trees as they took the dogs out for a run before supper. Sitting in the garden where the last of the sun zoned in between the arms of two cedar trees, waiting for supper, Tom felt that family life had never seemed more desirable. Camilla was like a flower come into bloom; every time he looked at her she seemed warmer and happier, her sharp edges erased, even her craggy features blurred and softened. She smiled and laughed as she had never done when he first knew her. Betty came out with a large teapot and mugs on a tray, and they sat in the sunspot, basking, tired, deeply happy in the way physical weariness can trigger, when brought about by something much enjoyed.

'I never felt like this after a day's accounting,' Fred said. 'Tired, but not like this — more, irritably tired, depressingly tired. Feeling tired like this is pure luxury.'

'When you've got everything straight and working, will it be enough?' Tom asked. 'Will boredom set in?'

'There's always something else, isn't there? You've got to attract people, there's a lot of competition. I see it as ongoing, growing out of this place, possibly, or expanding the building. If it were bigger, you could run summer schools — specialist, painting per-haps, or drama. And there's skiing in the winter, which gives one an edge in this region.'

'The rat-race brain is still at work, you see,' Betty said, smiling. 'The dog can't change its spots.'

'No. The fact we chose it — I didn't get made redundant, I wasn't forced into a new life-style — it makes it more important to succeed. With three children, we're always going to need the cash.'

'It's brave to choose out.'

'Or daft, I'm not sure.'

'Life can pass you by,' Betty said, 'While you're not making up your mind. You need to bend it your way, because if you wait for chance you might wait for ever.'

She was very earnest, pale blue eyes blinking behind her spectacles. She was totally without sex-appeal, without any sort of visual attraction, like a dry stick, but she had created a living home and sustained an enviable, thriving family. She was the total opposite to Jo. Tom wondered if she had chosen Fred, as some energetic, clear-headed girls tended to do, taking the initiative over an easy-going, kindly nature. He had sometimes suspected this of Jo, whom he had met at a party. He had been attracted to her, but it was she who had suggested they meet again. He, unlike Betty, had been allowing life — social life — to pass him by at the time, setting up his studio and nursing his first customers. He had not been a great one for the girls in any case, but Jo had managed him cleverly. He had never regretted it. Even when she wouldn't have a child, he had never wished he hadn't married her. With Camilla at his side, he could still think of Jo tenderly and with love.

Betty put the children to bed and they ate a large lamb casserole. There were no more guests and Fred played the piano — 'You can get a job in the local if all else fails,' Tom pointed out. They sang 'Clementine' and 'Home on the Range' and 'There is a Tavern in the Town'.

'Breakfast at six? Seven? Eight? Nine?' Betty enquired, laying the table again for the morning.

'Eightish would be reasonable,' Tom thought. He usually got up at six.

As it was, he was making love to Camilla at seven forty-five, and they were down twenty minutes late. There was a smell of burnt toast, Betty was singing in the kitchen, the radio was playing. Two children in striped pyjamas were playing Monopoly on the floor in the dining-room and one of the Labradors was carrying a large bone upstairs. Tom always remembered, afterwards, pausing in the doorway and tangibly absorbing the atmosphere of content — at his lot, the day ahead, the situation with Camilla, and this hospitable family. It was as strong as the smell of the toast.

'Coffee or tea?' Betty shouted.

'Coffee, please.'

He sat down with Camilla at the laid places, and in a moment Betty brought the coffee in a jug.

'Your name is Monk, isn't it? You said Monk?'

'That's right.'

'I thought when you said it, how unusual, and now, on the radio this morning there's another, Jo Monk, a headmistress.'

'On the radio? Why?'

The toasty content fled, and Tom wanted to shake Betty as she hesitated. Not given to panic, he knew it now.

'What is it?'

'Something rather horrible. A school trip, and two of the children drowned.'

'Oh Christ!'

Tom got up, nearly knocking the table over. Jo's dread seized him in exactly the same way, as if he had seen that empty deck too. Pure cold funk overwhelmed him. He shook visibly, and had to go to the window and clutch the sash, turning his back on the room, to get a hold of his senses.

'What is it?' Betty asked, alarmed. 'Is it a relation?'

She looked at Camilla's suddenly tight, white face.

'It's his wife,' Camilla said.

# 7

Nick rang for the police and they came in motor-launches; a helicopter came, the inshore lifeboat came. Jo was no longer in charge and gave up, gave in, with shaking relief.

'Who will tell them? The parents?'

'We — the police — will tell them. We have a lot of experience, I'm afraid. We know the best way to do it — although — ' The man shrugged. He was older, and kind, not sharp.

'With Daniel — with Daniel's mother — I must come too. Can you do that for me?'

'Perhaps.'

The moonlit river was dotted with lights, and voices carried on the still evening. Some of them sounded cheerful, a job of work. 'Get your fat arse out of the way, Arthur,' Jo heard, distant, from a small boat.

'Do bodies float?'

'Not always.'

'They could both swim, Daniel quite well.'

'The shore party will find them if they've made it that far.'

But they'd have been shouting, Jo thought, seeing all the commotion. The tide ran like a tiger on the top of the ebb.

Nick stayed by her side.

'Don't go to Daniel's mother,' he said. 'You can do no good. It's yourself you need to look after. You're in shock.'

Jo felt that nothing was quite real. She could not cope with believing the two children were dead. She thought one of the little boats — fat Arthur, perhaps — would return with them shortly. She sat wrapped in a blanket on the stern of the barge, watching the dark water, unaware of the comings and goings. The children were taken off in motorboats, and she did not question it. A whitefaced Penny Curtis took charge of them. Stevie went too. The barge became base for the search-party, and radio conversation crackled back and forth. Jo's teeth chattered.

'Here.' Nick brought her strong tea in his own thick mug. 'You can come back with me soon, to my mum. She'll look after you. It wasn't your fault, Jo. I'll tell them that. No one looked after 'em better than you.'

'It was my fault.'

'In that case, mine too. And Penny's and Norm's. You can't separate off and say it was yours.'

'They were my children.' Her voice was fierce. 'Not yours or Penny's or Norm's. It was my fault.'

'She'd best be taken home,' the policeman said. 'There's no more to be said at the moment. We'll send a message if there's any news.'

'Come on, Jo, you heard what he said.'

'We'll get a police car down here to take her, and she can go ashore in the inflatable, land on the beach. Is there anyone at home if we take you there, love? Your husband there?'

'He's in Scotland. I'll go to Ros, my friend.'

'I'll fix it.'

'We'll keep you informed. If we find anything.'

'The phone number — ' Jo gave it.

She went in the inflatable. They made Nick stay behind. 'You might be wanted. She'll be well looked after.'

Nick's blanket trailed over the pneumatic stern and Jo pulled it back round her, huddled and silent. The moon had been swallowed up by cloud and the smooth, fast water was now dark and cold. The lights were far away, the voices indistinguishable. Jo saw the two bodies, minnow-like, in her mind's eye, turning spreadeagled on the surface of the water, face-down, her dear Daniel and Kevin the scrambled-egg genius, their lives undone before they were scarcely started. What had they done? Norm said it was the bucket . . . 'That Kevin, I reckon, tried to fill

195

it. He wanted to try it. He asked me — it intrigued him, like, filling the bucket. It'd pull 'im in quite easy, specially if he didn't want to let go, didn't want to lose it, like, and get into trouble. And that other youngster, that Daniel, he might have jumped in after, thinking he could save him.' It was all in character, Kevin doing what he was told not to, Daniel helping, jumping after him on the spur of the moment. But nobody knew what had happened, it was only guessing. Jo was still shaking and icy-cold, although the air was mild. It was all a bad dream. If so to her, how so to Liz Weston? Jo could not contemplate Liz Weston without the ice binding her guts. She clutched the blanket.

'Easy does it, gel.' The lifeboatmen treated her like a child, handing her out on to a patch of hard beach, holding her arm as they walked up to the seawall. A police car had come across the grazing behind the wall and was waiting. Jo got in the back with a policewoman.

How kind, how terribly kind everyone was! It was worse than being abused. The Tranters would abuse her as she deserved. It might seem real when she met the Tranters. She might take it in then. She would take it in when she met Ann Forrester and Crispin

Grott. She wept. The policewoman put an arm round her.

Ros and Dave had apparently been told what had happened for they were at the door waiting, taking Jo into their arms, holding her, Ros weeping with her while Dave made the ubiquitous strong tea. The children were in bed and a fire was burning in the summer grate. Jo shivered and talked and wept and Ros sat close listening. Dave said he would go down to Liz Weston's and see if he could help out there; he was not afraid of emotional situations, a man who could rise to the occasion.

'I'll do whatever's necessary. She must have some relations or friends somewhere. But I won't leave her, don't worry. I'll stay the night if she needs me.'

They dissuaded Jo from going herself, and Ros got her to bed, half-stunned with a hot whisky.

'I want Tom,' Jo said, her last words before she fell asleep.

★   ★   ★

Liz Weston stood with her back to the pantry door and screamed. She held her arms out, palms against the wall, flung her head back and screamed. Dave walked in and saw the

197

policewoman's face. She was very young and had learned out of books and by lectures and not yet by experience. A constable, also young, the driver of the police car, stood by the door with his arms folded and his face stony with hatred of his job, useless as a cabbage.

'Are you a friend of hers?' the girl asked.

Dave explained who he was. They stood side by side, uncertain, knowing that Liz's violent reaction must burn itself out. She looked like a cornered animal, vicious and unpredictable, but when her frail body had spun its vehemence they were able to take her outstretched arms gently into theirs and guide her to a chair. The screams fell to sobs and eventually to gasps and whimpers. The constable made tea and found a bright electric fire which he plugged in; he fetched a blanket: he could carry out the statutory treatment for shock, all according to the book, but he had no words for bereaved women, only the puppet action. The girl was more willing to try but Liz was oblivious of her presence, wrapped in her wild grief. It was a matter of seeing her through, and they were willing to leave it to Dave, their initial duty completed.

They departed.

Dave stood staring out into the small dark

patch of garden. Lights shone in from neighbouring houses; two cats jumped over the fence; the bluish light of a television screen flickered from the house across the garden. Suburban life continued in its trivial pattern in spite of Liz now deciding she had nothing to live for. The cats yowled and somebody else's son was revving up a motorbike with an enthusiasm Daniel would not now know. Dave wondered what he would do if a policeman called to tell him his own Robert had died in an accident? It would take more than a cup of tea and the extra bar of the electric fire to comfort him, but one became used to anything in time, one adapted, one learned to live limbless, loveless, childless, given sufficient number of passing days. He sat across the kitchen table from the stricken Liz until her hysteria died, then guided her to her own sofa in the hutch-sized living-room, replugged the electric fire, retucked the blanket, pulled up a chair to sit beside her.

'Is there anybody you would like to come and stay with you? Any relations? I can ring them for you, whatever you want. Or I can stay, I don't mind.'

'No. I don't want anybody. There isn't anybody. There never was anybody, except Peter and Daniel.'

Fresh sobs shook her. From her white, swollen face her eyes swam dark with agony. Dave, who had parents, inlaws, brothers, sisters, aunts, uncles and cousins galore besides Ros and the children, tried to think of having nobody, and failed. It was beyond his imagination.

'A friend, a neighbour?'

'No. But you needn't stay. I'd rather be alone.'

'I'll stay. I'm perfectly happy to stay.'

She was shaking rather than trembling, and her hands and feet were cold as ice. He found a hot-water bottle and brought a duvet down from a bedroom and fussed around like a mother hen, his mind blanked out. It was something to be got through, endured, sat out; there was no getting round it. She did not look like sleeping for a long time. Perhaps he should call a doctor, and ask for sedatives, sleeping pills. He asked for her doctor's name, but she refused to tell him.

'I don't want pills, I won't take them. It won't make it go away, will it? They might find him quite soon. They'll come and tell me.'

She started to talk about Daniel, of his habits and likes and skills, the things he said, the teachers he liked, the errands he ran for her. He was like his father, Peter. Peter had been quiet, a bit shy, steady.

'What happened to Peter?'

'He died of cancer, when he was twenty-nine. We'd just moved here, got a mortgage on this place. He was an electrician, nothing very smart but he had plenty of work. People liked him. He thought the world of Daniel and me, never wanted to go out with other people — just us — just stay at home — '

She choked.

Christ, Dave thought, why her? What had she done to deserve it twice? Loving, content, simple — not bitchy and bored and cantankerous.

'How did you meet?'

'We met at the poly. He was a student and I was starting teacher-training. But we went out together and I got pregnant, so I gave up my course. I didn't mind, I was glad in fact, it was all I wanted, having the baby and loving Peter.'

'What about your parents?'

'They split up when I was small. My father went to America and my mother got another man — I hated him. They were really glad when I was old enough to leave home. Home was awful. I don't hear from them any more. Not even when Daniel was born, my mother didn't want to know. She had another baby of her own. I don't even know where she is now.'

Not worth looking for, from the sound of it, Dave thought.

It was hard to tell how strong or otherwise Liz was, whether — having now lost everything — she would stop looking to the past and make herself a new life, or whether she would go under completely. She was a frail-looking woman, slight and blonde and without anything striking in her looks. It was obvious from her home that it received a great deal of loving care; so had Daniel. What was there left? There must be more in life than the supermarket-till. Dave knew that much of Jo's concern was for the vulnerability of this woman. If he knew the Tranters, and he did, they would be ringing their lawyer by now. But Jo was less concerned about that side of the tragedy, in spite of its greater threat to herself.

There was no drink in the house, no knock-out pills. Dave managed to get Liz to take three aspirins and sat with her until she eventually fell into desperate sleep. He got another blanket from upstairs and rolled himself up in an armchair and dozed uncomfortably through the night.

★   ★   ★

Tom drove very fast, and Camilla realised that he was going to do the Spey valley to Essex without stopping. He said nothing at all. She had thought that as they drove they would talk the situation through, but by the time they got to the border she realised that this was not going to happen. Tom's face was so set and stern she could not broach his silence, only sit and nurse her shattered delusions of eternal bliss. Jo needed him. For the first time in their marriage Tom was being called upon to be a support to his stricken wife. His answer was crucifying in its rapidity and concern. He had packed up, paid and departed before Betty's bacon had cooled on the grill. Camilla, staring through the window at the rolling, sunwashed tops of the border hills flying past, could not believe that hopes could be obliterated with quite such savagery. She felt as if she had been physically shaken almost to uncon-sciousness, limp and bruised, and was upright still only by courtesy of the efficient seat-belt. When practical matters eventually overtook her stunned senses, she realised that she — unlike Tom — had no desire at all to go back home. In fact the thought of returning to her aunt's flat in Covent Garden filled her with such revulsion that she straightened up and cried out, 'Please let me get out! I don't want to go back!'

'You can't get out here,' Tom said.

'Somewhere then — anywhere — I'm not going home! You've got to, but I haven't!'

'That's true. I'm sorry. I didn't think. You said you wanted to come.'

She had thought he needed her support. She thought he would have had things to talk about, urgent and difficult. She had thought wrong.

'Yorkshire then — that place — that place we stayed at — I'll get out there! That'll do.'

'You'll have no car.'

'I don't want a car. I'm on holiday, aren't I? I can walk. It's a walking holiday, isn't it?'

She was scared and angry, angry at Tom's opting out. It was her life too. What was he doing to her? Hurry, hurry, she wanted to say, when he was already hurrying at considerable danger both to themselves and other road users. She wanted desperately to be rid of him, because of what he was doing to her. Dumping her.

'I can't talk,' he said. 'I don't know what to say. When I know what to say, I'll come back to you.'

He was no practised charmer, that was plain, and from that she must take comfort. When they got to the Yorkshire village where they had first stayed the night he stopped the car at the bottom of the lane where the B and B was. He helped her out with her small amount of luggage.

'Are you sure this is the best place for you?'

'Quite sure.'

It was a bland, still, beautiful afternoon, with the sheep bleating timelessly on the hillside fields. A small cluster of tents bloomed on the grass beside the river and the fragrance of wood burning floated across the road.

'I like it here.'

'There are worse places.'

Tom went back to the driving seat and slammed the door. He ran down the window.

'I'll get back to you, when I know what's happening.'

He drove off quickly, and the Porsche disappeared round the bend in the valley road. Camilla stood by her luggage like a hitch-hiker. She felt exhausted, as if she had been walking all day, and numb, and not quite all there. She walked slowly up the lane with her bag and knocked at the door of the Bed and Breakfast cottage. There was no answer. The house was empty. She left her bag in the porch and walked back down the lane to the road, remembering there was a sort of tea-room next door to the post office, a place for hikers, nothing grand. She was desperate for a cup of tea, anonymity — the place suited; ignored, she sat at her table in the window with a tin teapot before her and held her hands as if to warm them round the friendly teamug. Her hands were shaking. From having everything she had nothing, all in the space of a few hours. She could not help wondering if everything that had gone before was some sort of a fairy-story, and herself merely come awake. Life was back to normal, and she grounded, shot down, doomed as usual.

She dare not think of her love for Tom. Already she had discarded any hope of a future with him. Jo would lose her job, her beautiful independence, she would need Tom. Camilla needed Tom, but had learned to do without. Without. Without. The word had significance; her life was totally without — had she made it that way or was it something that dogged her? — her lack of ambition, her lack of drive, of guts, of friends, of lovers, of a home. Even the dog had died.

But for once she didn't cry. She finished her tea and went outside and walked up the hill where she had walked that first day with Tom. When she was on top and alone with the dales stretched all round her basking in the early evening sunshine, she flung out her arms and shouted, 'Tom! Tom! Tom!' with all her strength. Her voice was puny in the great space. 'Tom! Tom! I love you!'

Far away on the next moor a curlew answered her cry. A cool breeze smoothed her burning face. There was nobody in the world to be seen in any direction for as far as the eye could see.

★   ★   ★

Tom got home to find no sign of Jo nor her car. He was just going into the house when another car shot into the drive and pulled up beside his own in a flurry of gravel. A man got out, obviously in a towering rage. He was youngish, well-fleshed, and smartly dressed.

'Where is she?' he shouted at Tom. 'Where's the bloody murderer? Your bloody wife I'm talking about.'

Tom gathered who it was, but the attitude hardly stirred his sympathy. He said nothing, waiting. Tranter came up to the doorstep and faced him, breathing heavily.

'I've just come from the mortuary, identifying the body. My boy, my little lad. And where's the bloody woman who was supposed to be in charge of them, supposed to be looking after them — whose idea it all was in the first place? Your bleeding wife? You find her for me, mate, and I'll tell her she's got to answer for it! I'm going to sue her all the way, I'll hound her out of business — I'll make her life hell like she's made life hell for me — '

He was incoherent, breathing heavily, his grief possibly laced with alcohol. While Tom was taking in his aggression and wondering whether he was about to be physically assaulted, two young men appeared from round the side of the house and approached eagerly.

'Can I have a word, Mr Monk? Mr Tranter? I'm from the *Daily* — '

'The *East Anglian Recorder* — '

They flashed Press-cards. Tranter rounded on them.

'I can tell you a thing or two! I'll tell you what I know about Mrs bleeding Monk for a start — '

Tom opened the door with his key and slipped inside. One of the reporters went to put his foot in but Tom was too quick for him. Tranter hammered on the door but the pressmen started talking, and took him away down the drive where they stood in a huddle. Tom went blindly into his house, shaken by such venom. He had guessed already that things were going to be bad for Jo from the Tranter department, but had stupidly not expected the Press. No wonder she had departed if reporters had been knocking at the door.

He rang Ros.

'Yes, she stayed here. At the moment she's at an emergency meeting of the governors — as many as they could rake together considering it's holiday time. She wants you, Tom — thank God you heard the news. Why don't you go down to the school and pick her up? She'll be so relieved to see you! She's in a pretty bad state — you can imagine — '

'Yes, I'll go down. Okay, thanks.'

'Come back here, if you like. Feel free.'

'There are reporters hanging around here. And Tranter. I might take you up on that.'

'Yes, you're welcome.'

Tom rang off. The reporters were still outside, talking to Tranter, but by the time Tom had changed out of his walking clothes into something more suitable and had a quick wash they had all departed. He went out and drove down to the school. Jo's car was in the car-park. Tom parked beside it and sat for a bit, biting his nails. He felt suddenly very tired, and actually dozed off for a second or two. He was awoken by some young boys coming from the fish and chip shop, larking and shouting, and dropping greasy paper across the road. He watched with a sense of irritation, aware of a deep foreboding without remembering what had happened or why he was outside the school. It was a golden evening, windless, and the bland modern buildings stared at him across the paved, littered, architect's space. But as he looked at them another vision came to his mind, a very recent imprint almost violent in its effect, of standing on the top above Loch Einich and seeing the blue haze of the receding Cairngorms above and beyond. The happiness of that moment was sharp as a spear, but the memory passed instantly and left only the awful taste of reality. He groaned out loud.

He got out of the car and picked up the fish and chip papers, stuffing them into the litter-basket. He crossed the car-park into the school grounds and peered into the window of Jo's office. It was empty but through the open door he could see the governors' meeting going on in the classroom opposite. He could see old Motley, the chairman, listening intently to someone out of Tom's sight, and Ann Forrester leaning forward across her infant's table with a look on her face like a greedy child watching the last slice of cake.

Tom went in through the door and down the corridor. He opened the classroom door and stood there briefly. Motley looked up, recognising him.

'Excuse me — just to say — ' He saw Jo across the tables, nodded, and said to her, 'I'll wait in your office till you're through.'

'Tom!'

Jo managed to sit still, but her relief was palpable in the room.

'Sorry to disturb you.'

Motley smiled kindly and said, 'Glad you're back, old chap.'

He was a public-spirited, retired civil servant, finished with commuting, and grasping such minor honours as chairman of school governors to keep his talents alive in his reluctant retirement — one of the old school to whom Ann Forrester was radically opposed. He regularly punctured her opposition with impeccably phrased hatred. He adored Jo and supported her in everything she did. Long may it be so, thought Tom, closing the door. She was going to need friends.

He went to her office and sat in the customer's chair. He was always slightly surprised to discover Jo's femininity in her office, the patchworkery bias and sentimental pictures. Even when tidied up for the holidays it showed. She tailored such excesses at home to his austerity; he wondered if he restricted her too much. Perhaps one of her desired package holidays on a hot beach would be the very thing after this miserable interlude. But the prospect of it to him was unendurable. All the same, she would need every bit of sympathy and support he could manage during the next few weeks. How much had it been her fault — apart from going at all?

'It wasn't! It wasn't!' she wept in his arms ten minutes later. 'I couldn't have done more to see that they were safe! It was all a stunning success until — oh, Tom! Oh, Tom, thank God you're here! I've longed for you! Did the police find you?'

'I heard it on the radio.'

'The radio? Oh, the reporters — they're everywhere!'

'I know, I've met them. They're at home. And Mr Tranter. You haven't said anything, have you, not to any of them?'

'No, not a thing, only to Ros and Dave. Dave warned me. Old Motley's getting me a lawyer. But I don't need protecting — I didn't do anything wrong!'

'All the same, they drowned.'

'I know. I was in charge. I know.'

'What happened?'

Jo told him, exactly as she remembered it . . . that long, long second on the empty deck, and looking at the tide swirling past the rudder . . . she started shivering all over again.

'Don't, Jo! Don't!' Tom hugged her, appalled.

'And Daniel! That woman — all she has! Of them all, Daniel, the best . . . and Kevin made scrambled eggs — '

'Jo, stop it.'

'She screamed and screamed, Dave said.'

'Yes.'

He held her close, looking over her head. Through the glass panel in the door he could see the meeting carrying on with its discussion now that she had left them. Ann Forrester was talking, very animated. He could see her lips pecking away, the excitement in her eyes.

'Come on,' he said to Jo. 'I'll take you home. I won't leave you, I promise.'

In the middle of the night, lying awake, Jo turned to Tom and said, 'Do you think I'll lose my job?'

Tom turned over and put his arm over her shoulders.

'No such luck — for me, I mean. Why should you? The inquest will show that it was an accident — a true accident, something you could hardly have foreseen. Those parents gave permission for their children to go, after all. Beyond handcuffing them all together, you could hardly have watched them more responsibly, I would have said.'

'I keep telling myself that.'

'You have witnesses. Penny and Nick. Stevie. Norm. Kevin Tranter was far more likely to have got drowned in the creek, I would have thought, before your expedition ever got under way. What happened was freakish bad luck.'

'People have got to have someone to blame. There's only me. Newspapers — interviews on the television, you know — they always try to lay blame somewhere.'

'It's their job. Easy with hindsight.'

'They will blame me.'

'You've your record to set beside what anybody says.'

'But that's boring and dull. No one will care about that.'

'Anything going well is boring to the media, use your sense. Sudden death is always fascinating. All those funerals on the news ... easy television, get it all set up beforehand, zoom in on the widow, the parents — great stuff. And blame — it makes other people feel good, self-righteous — I wouldn't do a thing like that. They only watch it on television, never get their arses out of an armchair to do anything risky themselves — never stick their necks out far enough to get sniped at. Don't worry, Jo — your record's too good to let this floor you.'

In the dark and silent early morning before dawn the worst fears always rose their heads. Jo was soothed by Tom's support. But Tom lay on his back remembering Camilla and what he had said to her. He remembered the look on her face, all her sharp edges lost in scorching, radiant love and happiness. Christ! What was he doing to her? What was she feeling, alone in the bedroom with the farmer's dog barking at a fox, the stars blinking above the moors? She should have come back with him to London, where he could reach her. An ocean lay between them now, not just the miles down the A1. He did not know how, or if, he was ever going to touch her again.

\* \* \*

'What are you going to do today?' Dave asked Ros at breakfast.

'Well, thank God Tom came back. I haven't got Jo to worry about quite so much. I ought to go and see Liz Weston, I suppose.'

'Those people seemed to know what to do. She's not alone.'

Dave had enlisted the help of a community Help-Your-Neighbour scheme which had been set up in the new town. Neighbours in this case had been imported; Liz's own neighbours hadn't seemed overhelpful. She hadn't been a wow at making friends. But the community lot had the official stamp of helpfulness, bossy and bracing, and Dave had been relieved to hand over. He hadn't wanted to bring her back with him, which is what Ros had wanted. Personally he found Liz Weston totally and utterly depressing; her complete capitulation in the face of catastrophe, although perfectly understandable, made him feel both angry with her and guilty with himself. He did not want to think about her, much less have her at home. He preferred Tranter's reaction. If one could not have dignity and courage in the face of grief, better rage than weakness.

'The first shock has been digested. It will all now wend its weary way through the courts or wherever — the Education Committee — God, poor Jo. She's not very patient, and she's going to need patience.'

'She's got Tom. He's a rock.'

'Yes. Not the exciteable type. Steady, just what she needs.'

It was a coincidental result of the arrangement of the houses where they lived that the Taylor kitchen looked out over the Grott back garden and into the Grott kitchen. The respective families always drew their curtains at dusk to shut each other out.

216

Anyone else and it wouldn't have mattered, in Ros' opinion, but she had no desire for the earnest Crispin to see her slaving over the washing-up after hours. But at breakfast they had become accustomed to glimpses of each other over the toast, too early for pretence, and it was as Ros went to the window to pour the remains of the teapot into her geraniums that she caught sight of fascinating developments taking place across the lawns. Ann Forrester had arrived in the Grott kitchen and was being entertained to coffee.

'My God, look at that! The vultures at work. She's not losing much time.'

'What are you talking about?'

Ros explained. She went and fetched her bird-watching binoculars from the hall cupboard and got down on her knees, focusing them through the rampant geraniums.

'God, Ros, it's unseemly in a schoolmistress!' Dave was amused.

'If I could lip-read! She's rabbiting away, eyes on stalks. And Lorna's got to go to work but can't bear to leave darling Crispin alone with all-consuming Ann.'

'What are you looking at, mummy?'

The youngest Taylor had arrived for his breakfast, ferreting in the pantry for cornflakes.

'She's studying human behaviour,' Dave said.

'Spying.'

'Yes, spying.'

'I wish I had a bug under their table.' Ros put the glasses away, having summed up the situation. 'You do see what they're at, don't you? Getting Crispin into Jo's job?'

'Yes, I do see.'

'Over my dead body!'

'I doubt if you'll have a say in it. Ann Forrester is only one governor, after all, the only one — I imagine — who won't support Jo. Old Motley and Co won't let her down.'

'She's a snake, the worst type. A trouble-maker, wants to make her mark, using the job to up herself. She has no idea of supporting, bettering the school, only of carping and sniping and — '

'Don't get wound up! The world's full of 'em. Two a penny. Thank your stars you've only one under your skin! Think of me tonight, playing Rachmaninov under that nutcase from Outer Siberia — he's another one who wants to be noticed, believe me. You can't take Jo's troubles on your shoulders, Ros. That's why you've never applied to be a head yourself, remember?'

He went to work and left Ros scowling over the washing-up. Crispin was still closeted with Ann Forrester, talking, talking. Last night he had accosted Ros over the fence when she was getting the washing in, and asked her what she knew about the tragedy. He knew Jo had spent the night with her. He had been full of concern, shocked — in fact, perfectly sympathetic and likeable until, just as Ros picked up the washing basket and made to end the conversation, he said, 'Of course, I always maintained it was a dangerous expedition right from the start. It was unwise to go on the water.'

'It's unwise to cross the road, Cris. Five thousand people get killed every year on the road.'

'Yes, well, that is something society accepts.'

Ros hated people who talked about society. His smug and inconsequential remark infuriated her. She flounced away with her washing, hating the unremarkability of the man, his concern with all the small things in life. He would never get run over; he looked all ways several times and never drove at more than forty-five miles an hour. He never ran, his mother having told him the dangers at an early age. He would become a headmaster and bore generations of children to tears. The damage would be incalculable. Life was like that. All the best teachers got promoted to be inspectors or administrators and never taught again, but Crispin would go on until he retired, grinding the young into literacy and numeracy like a board school dame, and keeping them safe. Perhaps that was what the parents all wanted in the end, the long plod rather than the exciting ride. Her heart ached for Jo who would find being criticised terribly hard.

But the children were dead all right. Their bodies had been found washed up together on the mud flats at low water, unmarked. They had been taken to the mortuary and examined by a pathologist; the coroner had been informed and a date for the inquest was being decided. Behind the scenes fraught meetings were being held by the education hierarchy, both official and unofficial, spurred by the recriminations of John Tranter and the particularly pugnacious lawyer he had appointed. Jo, after a private interview with someone on the legal side of the Education Committee whom she had never met before, was thereafter set aside, her case discussed out of her presence, not only in council chamber but in teachers' houses, on summer courses, on television, on the street and in the newspapers. Hard news was sparse and the emotions of the tragedy were press-worthy; the human content was rich: the vociferous

Tranter, beautiful young headmistress, distraught, childlike widow, and camera-friendly Thames barge. The two journalists Tom had discovered on the doorstep on his return home swelled to a continuing embarrassment of callers at all times of the day. Jo went out, but found no rest in the school or in the neighbourhood, finding normal acquaintances confused by her presence, not knowing how, or even whether, to frame condolences and appearing to her jaundiced eyes to be hostile and blaming. Her only safe retreat — Ros's house — was soon discovered by journalists.

'You must go away for a bit,' Ros said. 'It's hopeless for you here.'

Jo somehow felt it was a just punishment, part of the suffering required of her, as Liz must suffer, and the Tranters. Ros had kept her strenuously apart from Liz Weston, feeling that Liz's capitulation would undo Jo.

'Tell Tom to take you somewhere — new faces, who don't know. Obscurity. Just for a week or two.'

'I shall have to be here for the inquest.'

'They haven't even fixed a date yet! You know how slowly it all grinds. You can keep in touch.'

'Not abroad.'

'No. All right. Tom will think of some-where.'

Tom did.

'I stayed in a place in Scotland. Nice people. I was there when I heard the news. It's perfect for a retreat — there's a very good weather forecast for the north for the next few weeks — all the best weather's going to Scotland, so why not us too?'

It was a calculated risk. Even if she found out about Camilla — perhaps the children would mention her, although he knew Fred and Betty would not — it was going to have to come out some time, if Jo chose to go on denying him his child. Camilla, Tom calcu-lated, should be back home and back at work by now, but when he rang, her aunt said she was still away, and she hadn't heard from her.

'I'm a bit worried about her, to tell you the truth. It's not like her not to let me know what she's doing.'

Auntie didn't know Camilla hadn't gone away alone. She knew Tom as an acquain-tance, who had come to the flat after he had been mugged. Tom rang off. He too was worried about Camilla, and had been ever since she had left him so precipitously in Yorkshire. Her aunt's news did nothing to allay his doubts. He had never intended to ditch her just like that. Once it was sorted out with Jo he was going to talk it through with Camilla — what the outcome was going to be, he had no idea at all. His affair was in an unholy tangle.

'You're not going to make me climb mountains all day? I feel terribly tired, although I haven't been doing anything except sit about.'

'No, of course not. But it's away from it all — you've had no peace since it happened. You'll get peace up there.'

'I shall have to leave my address — a phone number — with that lawyer . . . ' She spoke in a distracted, edgy way that had become characteristic since the accident. Her confidence in herself was shattered; she looked ill and had lost almost a stone in weight.

'The rest will do you good — you really do need to wind down. Even before this happened you were due for a holiday, after all.'

Tom felt genuinely protective, and remembered that it was Camilla who had made him feel this way in the past — needed, a strong shoulder to cry on — it was strange to find Jo needing him.

'I'm going to lose my job,' she said. The tears slipped down her cheeks.

'Jo, don't!'

Tom put his arms round her and held her

closely. They sat down on the sofa together and she wept copiously, burying her face in the front of his pullover. He stroked her hair and gazed over her head into the too-perfect sitting-room, untrammelled by human child, at the expensive stereo gear, the row of compact discs, the pale, clean furniture and the neat, unobstrusive bookcase with its uncommitted books (*Rebecca*, dog-eared, *The Drove Roads of Scotland*, *Beethoven's Letters*, ten Dick Francis's) . . . something has got to change, he thought. I can't bear this any more. Jo's catastrophe was going to change it. She was going to lose her job and have a baby instead. He kissed her gently, friendlily.

'I do love you, Jo.'

He did too. And Camilla as well. Camilla! Jesus, what a crook he was! He had called in the church and listened to the choir, but she had not been amongst them. A soprano is missing, he had thought sadly, like the title of a crime novel. He had known she wouldn't be there even before he had gone through the door into the silent, familiar ambience of what he thought of as 'his' church. Nobody knew where she had gone. He had rung the Bed and Breakfast in Yorkshire to see if she was still staying there, and Mrs Haythorn told him she had stayed two nights only, and then gone. She had paid up and taken her luggage with her. Tom had asked, on an offchance, if anyone had perhaps taken the cottage across the road, but Mrs Haythorn said no. She thought it was sold to a man from Wolverhampton. Tom was beginning to wonder if her disappearance was serious — but surely she had known he would get in touch with her again? He had promised. She wouldn't do anything stupid, surely? If he went back to Scotland with Jo, he would feel it his duty to see her parents and make enquiries.

'Can you come too, or have you got to stay and work?' Jo asked, as the weeping came under control. She was not, like Camilla, a weeper, and despised herself for showing such lack of control. She sat up and wiped her face briskly, and pushed back her hair.

'Yes. August's a dead month in the office, you know that. If anything important comes up, Terry can give me a ring. Start getting your things together. The sooner you get away from here the better.'

He rang Fred and Betty and told them the situation. They said they would keep a room for them, to stay as long as they liked; they would do all they could.

Awkwardly, before ringing off, Tom said, 'Just for the record, I stayed with you on my own, when I was up before. Not to worry too much, but for the time being . . . she's got enough worries.'

'Yes, fine, we understand.'

How could they, he wondered? He didn't understand what he was doing himself half the time.

He felt as relieved as Jo to be heading away from home again. Just before they left Jo was given a date for the inquest on the two boys. It was three weeks ahead, at the end of August. She wouldn't talk about it, but having an actual date was a relief. The timing, Tom thought, was just right — long enough away for her to wind down, not too far away to become an ordeal.

The weather was soft and warm, the sky clear. The roads were full of holiday traffic, carefree people with cars full of children and dogs and push-chairs. Jo and Tom felt set apart. Tom stopped at a nice hotel for lunch, wanting Jo to have the best of everything. It was afternoon by the time they came into Yorkshire, and Tom took the road through the valley where he had stayed with Camilla, unable to stay away. 'A scenic route,' he said to Jo. 'We're not in a hurry.' He was sick with himself, yet had to drive slowly, slow down as they came to the bridge over the stream and the turning that led to the pub. A quick glance showed him the cottage for sale, somnolent and dilapidated in the afternoon sun, untouched; the cows were still on the hillside, and two hikers, sweaty and red-faced, sat by the river with their rucksacks opened, cutting hunks of bread and cheese. The hills basked in the sunshine.

'Nice spot,' he said.

Jo did not answer.

He put his foot on the accelerator and zoomed on up the valley to the motorway beyond, but felt very disturbed. If Camilla had truly disappeared, what had become of her? It would not be difficult to walk into the hills and find a place where no one would ever find a huddled body — not, at least, until it was too late. If she was technically missing, he was the only person who knew why. Was she technically missing? He had no idea. As far as he knew, no one had told the police that she had disappeared.

If he were to be absolutely practical, Camilla disappearing should be a problem off his back. Now that Jo needed him, and might possibly lose her job and agree to have a baby, Camilla was extraneous to needs. Practical as that line of thought appeared, it did not cheer him at all. He knew he was too far in it with Camilla; he thought about her all the time, even while he was loving Jo.

'What's wrong?'

'Sorry. Just dreaming.'

The Porsche had slowed so that on the winding road several cars had built up behind him. Tom put his foot down and roared back to his normal speed, rapidly leaving them behind.

'We'll stop fairly early, and get a good dinner. Give ourselves time to choose. We're getting on for halfway.'

'How about Durham? Or is that too soon? I love Durham.'

'Fine.'

By the time they reached Fred and Betty's place the following afternoon Jo had cheered up and was taking an interest. Tom was banking on her getting on with Betty, and watched keenly as he introduced them and the two women shook hands. He thought Betty was Jo's type, a sort of intellectual Ros, with strong opinions. Betty, although the perfect mother, found her children a tie and a drag on her own ambitions, and was anxious to get the youngest to school, and get on with her own living. She wasted little time, helping Fred with the decorating, making curtains and the children's clothes, and in the evening relaxing with improving novels and uplifting newspapers. In Chalfont St Giles, she must have been on committees, Tom thought, and run coffee mornings for good causes. She was admirable and endearing, of the strain that raised the empire, now outmoded. Her new home probably suited her better, where she could give rein to her pioneering characteristics. Certainly she seemed happy.

After shaking hands, she gave Jo a kiss and said, 'I am so sorry about what's happened. I do sympathise with your situation, believe me — I can just imagine what you must be going through. We want you to do whatever you want here, exactly what you feel — stay in bed all day if you like, or cry, or scream, no making polite conversation. Think of it as a bolt-hole. We really do want you to feel quite free.'

After all the hedging and embarrassed fudging that Jo had met with amongst her neighbours and acquaintances at home, Betty's straightforward grasping of the nettle came as a relief, and Tom saw her respond warmly. He himself felt awkward at greeting her again, having last been under her roof with Camilla, but she gave him no hard moments. She took them up to a different bedroom from the one he had shared with Camilla. It looked out over the front lawn where the friendly deckchairs were set out round the iron garden table and the dogs were being teased by two of the children. Tom watched them. The child thing flared in him suddenly and unexpectedly, with a sharp hurt. Nothing was changed in the way he felt; even in his concern for Jo now, he knew that the best thing that could happen as far as he was concerned was that she should lose her job. He could not say it. He was as two-faced as they come, and not proud of the way his mind worked. Thank God one's thoughts were one's own. He was not in the habit of giving much away. Mountains, he thought, looking up at the horizon, I need you. Again.

'You're not going to make me go climbing with you?'

'No.'

Jo slept heavily and the next morning Tom went alone, not the way he had gone with Camilla. But the calming mountains no longer calmed. Every where he looked he saw Camilla, and was afraid for her. His guilt was as bad as Jo's. Camilla had bloody loved him, with all the excessive passion of her strange, inhibited nature, and he had slammed the gates in her face. If he had been Terry he could have shrugged and laughed, but he could not even forget her, much less laugh. When he was back at Fred and Betty's he had to cover up; if he looked worried his worries must be for Jo and the outcome of the inquest which were, in fact, far less pressing in his mind.

The second evening, after Jo and Betty had gone to bed, Fred said he would take the dogs out.

'It's a super night. Want to come?'

They took the path up the glen in the half-twilight. An almost full moon was shining high over the hillside at the top of the valley, and Tom pictured the view from the top and the feel of it — a night for a sleeping-bag up there, and the stars at hand for company. He had done it many times and smelled the dewfall, shivering, and known the mystery, the essence of living. But other people did without, and thrived.

When they got back to the house, Fred said, quite directly, 'Does your wife know about Camilla?'

Tom found it easy to tell him, a relief, in fact, to share his troubles, like a woman's column.

'It's her disappearing that is the real worry. If I knew she hadn't done anything silly, I'd feel a lot better.'

'Why don't you see if her parents have heard from her? I know where their garage is, if that's any help. You needn't say you're her lover, for God's sake, just an old London friend passing this way, lost touch and all that.'

Tom had known he must do this, but didn't relish digging up families. He had learned to do without families, including one of his own.

Taking Fred's directions, he headed for the garage a few days later, when Jo decided to go with Betty to take the children swimming. It was some five miles away, a modest enough place on a road that had obviously become a lot busier since the garage was originally built. It was an isolated position, not a particularly prepossessing place in which to pass a childhood. A ginger-headed teenager served him, and took his money in silence.

Not much encouraged, Tom said, 'I'm an old friend of Camilla Hastings — do you know where she is these days? I've rather lost touch . . . just passing, thought I'd enquire.'

'I dunno. Ask her mum — she's in the shop.'

He jerked his head towards the accessory-cum-sweets shed that stood behind the pumps. Tom went across and opened the door. Behind the till a middle-aged woman was doing the accounts. She was an older Camilla, with the same craggy nose and springing dark hair, but her face had a worn and bitter expression, and she was dully dressed in drab, not too clean skirt and anorak and gumboots. She looked up without a smile.

Tom repeated his old-friend-just-passing enquiry, while pretending to choose a snack from the sweet counter.

'If you come from London, I daresay you'll see more of her than we do. She doesn't come this way any more.'

'Has she written to you?'

'She doesn't write, hardly ever.'

'You haven't heard from her lately then?'

'No.'

Tom was not surprised Camilla had shaken the dust of home from her heels. He bought a Mars bar and departed, the woman not interested in either his enquiry or her own daughter.

But the encounter only served to deepen his depression and anxiety, confirming that absolutely nobody had heard from Camilla since she had left Mrs Haythorn's Bed and Breakfast.

He told Fred.

'Do I tell the police? She's certainly gone missing.'

'I don't see that it would do a lot of good. She's entitled to disappear, after all. What good would it do to put out her description as a missing person, a photo and all that? She's a free agent.'

He was relieved when the time came to go home. His idea for Jo had worked too well; it was now himself who needed rehabilitating.

They left a few days before the inquest was scheduled. Both Betty and Fred were genuinely sorry to see them go, and begged them to come back again — 'Soon, whatever happens.'

'Funny,' Jo said, as they drove away, 'How it is — out of all the thousands of people you live with and see every day, how few you actually really hit it off with. When you do meet them — like Betty — it's so rare, it's fantastic. It makes you wonder about all the others there are, all over the place, I suppose, but you're never going to meet them. What a waste!'

'Life's like that.'

'Like what?'

'Chancy. That you met Betty because that's the B and B we just happened to choose that night.'

There was a long, long silence.

Tom knew she had noticed. We instead of I. He had assiduously avoided making that mistake all the last fortnight and now, when the strain was over and they had left the danger area, he had fallen into the trap in almost his first sentence. He drove down the narrow, twisting road through the forest, concentrating hard.

After two or three miles, Jo said, 'I knew, actually.'

'What?'

'That you were with someone else. One of the children let it out. Quite innocently, of course.'

After another mile or two, in which Tom digested this information, he asked, with genuine interest, 'Were you surprised?'

'Yes, I was actually. Especially when I found out who it was.'

'How did you do that?'

'I asked him.'

She was a headmistress, after all.

'The last person, I would have thought, to appeal to you.'

Tom did not know what to say next. Jo was speaking quite rationally, apparently without venom or distress, which somehow seemed to put him at a disadvantage.

'I suppose it's the mother thing . . . why you've found someone else? Because I won't have a baby?'

'That's what started it, yes.'

'Well, that's fair, I suppose.'

'You don't seem terribly upset.'

'I knew, after you'd been to see your mother and came back all lit up about your father being an actual monk, and you said

235

then — you really did want one . . . I saw that as an ultimatum, I suppose. And when I refused then, I knew it was on the cards that you would leave me. I had considered it. So I can't throw a wobbly now, can I?'

Another long silence. They came to the main road and Tom filtered in and quickly across to overtake.

'What if this inquest goes against you, and you lose your job?'

'You mean will I have a baby?'

'Yes, I mean that.'

'I can't answer that one. Not now.'

But the look had come into her face that was familiar to him, the jut of the jaw and the expression of pain, a bleak reaction to the image of the so-called joy of motherhood. That expression hurt him equally. Nothing was changed.

# 8

When they got home, Jo found the house unsympathetic and cold, and migrated immediately to her school office on the pretext of wanting to look up some notes of the last governors' meeting. She wanted to sit behind her desk again and feel back where she belonged, the familiar children's paintings looked down on her. She wanted the smell of polish and chalk and the suspended silence of the empty school cocooning her, welcoming her back. Her school. Across the lawns and flowerbeds people went about their business in the town square, not interested in her traumas. A dog peed against the gate-post and one of her third years went past on a pair of roller skates. Nothing changed. If she went, she would quickly be forgotten.

She knew her mood was unhealthy, and made the effort to leave and drive on to Ros's house, to find out what she might have missed while she was away.

Ros welcomed her with a great hug and a kiss.

'Oh, you look so much better! What a good idea of Tom's, taking you up there! You're quite brown! Come and sit down, I'll make some coffee.'

'Tell me all the news. I've got to catch up.'

'Oh, nothing. It's all the same as when you left. Much muttering behind closed doors and Mr Tranter trying to get Liz Weston on his side and failing. She's rallied quite well, you'll be pleased to hear — well enough to repulse Tranter, at any rate. She's turned down the offer of going along with his lawyer, doesn't want to complain, she says.'

'Tranter's going to complain? Sue, you mean?'

'Only if the result of the inquest gives him a chance. Which it won't, so don't worry about it. Without the support of the other parent involved, he's going to look a bit silly, isn't he?'

'Blame! And if I'd left Kevin off the list, he'd have kicked up as much fuss! He'd have come round to see me, asking why.'

'Don't worry about him. He's not going to get a chance to say anything at the inquest. He'll only be called to give evidence of identification, that's all.'

'What he doesn't understand is that we're on the same side! He blames me, I blame myself, yet in God's name I don't see how I could have foreseen such an accident. Yet I can't go and talk to him, say I'm sorry, because the lawyer says I'm not to see him.'

'Just as well, in my opinion. When the evidence is given, no one will find you at fault, Jo, I'm sure. Thank God it will be over in a couple of days.'

'It will never be over. And what will happen to me? What will the Education Committee decide? It's only because it's holiday time that they haven't suspended me yet.'

Ros knew Jo had the loyal backing of the governors, save for Ann Forrester, but education committees were notoriously nervous when litigation was in the air. Ros reassured her, pressed her with tea and homemade cake, and Jo sat back and lapped up the warmth and familiarity. Tom's news about Camilla was locked in the back of her mind and she would not let it out. She could not tell Ros. She did not want to think about it until later. It was an abyss, to be confronted when there was time for clear thinking. It seemed at the moment only half as important as the inquest, yet if she stopped to think about this assessment of her marriage she knew it would appall her.

She told Ros about Betty and her new friendship. Sitting in Ros's old armchair — Ros's interiors were well-used and untidy and extraordinarily homely — she was strongly aware of her affection for this setting.

The atmosphere of the house was much more sympathetic than that of her own. That had been true of Fred and Betty's place too. It was somehow to do with children and dogs and cats and a certain amount of chaos, people doing their own thing and the evidence all around: unfinished knitting and Dave's musical scores in an untidy heap, a model aeroplane and the smell of glue mixing with the smell of newly-made apricot jam. How rare and antiseptic was the atmosphere of her own home by contrast. Yet she did not desire these things that made for homeliness: children and domesticity. She hated making jam. She never made jam. What did she want? She was completely disorientated.

When she went home, late in the evening, Tom was watching television and drinking. He rarely drank at home. They neither of them had anything to say to each other and Jo went to bed.

★   ★   ★

'Mummy, you're always spying!'

The following day Ros's eldest found her behind the geraniums with the binoculars.

'What's old Grott doing now?'

What indeed?

Grott was talking to Ann Forrester and

Stevie. Stevie? What on earth was Stevie doing there?

'You're wicked.'

Ros retreated, and put the binoculars back in their case.

'You're quite right. One finds out things one does not want to know. Spying is a no-good occupation.'

But what was Grott finding out from Stevie? The mind boggled.

★　★　★

Tom drove Jo to the inquest, which was scheduled for ten-thirty, Court Three. Ros sat in the back of the car, trying to be cool and quiet. She had not mentioned finding Stevie in Grott's kitchen. She tried to say nothing at all, aware that all paths were fraught with danger, and herself not the soul of tact at the best of times. Tom and Jo were equally quiet, and Ros could feel a tension between them which she felt had nothing at all to do with the current situation. Tom was at his most distant, unsmiling.

It was very warm, muggy, and the town was crowded. There was nowhere to park. Tom drove round and round several times before finding an awkward spot in a residential road. The courts park was already full, probably

241

— Ros thought — with the cars of the nosey-parkers coming to see Jo put through the hoops. There were several members of the Press milling around and a man with a video camera rudely zoomed in as they approached the swing doors of the court-house. Several reporters shouted questions at Jo, but she said nothing, advised tersely by Tom. It was what they had all seen a thousand times on television and seemed utterly familiar — the scuffles and elbowing, the intimate, crude questions tossed like buns to a zoo bear, and their own ducking into the blessed revolving door to get out of the crush.

They made their way up a wide stone staircase to the floor above where the courtrooms opened off a wide, crowded corridor. There were a lot of people about, presumably the sued and the sueing and all their attendants. The doors to the court-rooms opened and shut regularly, people coming in and out; disembodied voices called for various people by name, and kindly ushers directed the confused and the ignorant. They found Court Three but they were early and the inquest before the one that concerned them was still in progress. Nick and Norm, looking abnormally clean and well-dressed, were waiting outside, and there were some governors and Education

Committee members. They were all mingling uneasily, with a false, bright civility which reminded Ros of a congregation collecting outside the doors of a crematorium. Jo had to go through with it but she — thank God — was only a spectator and she decided to escape to the public gallery at once. A glimpse of the Tranters at the far end of the corridor sped her on her way.

The gallery was up another flight of the stairs. When she got to the door she found Crispin hovering outside with Ann Forrester at his side.

'Good morning, Ros.'

He looked uneasy, as if he knew what Ros suspected. Proof of subversion was at his side, smiling her tight, frosty smile.

'Good morning, Mrs Taylor.'

'Good morning. Are you going to sit up here? I think you're entitled to be in the court proper, as one of the governors.'

'It's going to be very crowded — so many Press here. It's only a small court. I thought it would be more comfortable up here.'

She was proved right, as usual. The gallery was already nearly full and the Press benches below were crowded, although the previous case was still being heard. They slithered in and Ros sat in a row behind Cris and Ann. She did not want to be associated with them.

Ann Forrester should be below with her
fellow governors, in support, not whispering
with Cris in the gallery. Ros sat looking out of
the high sun-washed windows, trying to calm
the rages that were clashing in her breast
— instinctive rages, she had to acknowledge,
not rooted in common sense. The glimpse of
Mr Tranter, his large, once florid face now
taut and white with bitterness and hatred,
had reminded her of the less savoury aspects
of human nature. One could only assume
(kindly) that grief took the man this way. All
the patience and skill Jo had used with his
difficult son over the years now counted for
nothing, nor was Jo's own genuine grief over
the boy acknowledged. His own feelings were
paramount. Aggressive and greedy, he was
unable to aspire to finer feelings in this
tragedy. He must kick out and blame. One
should feel pity for him, but Ros felt only
disgust.

The court cleared after the coroner
announced the verdict on the preceding case,
a suicide, and started to fill with parents,
governors, witnesses and interested parties,
nearly all of whom Ros knew and yet who
seemed unfamiliar in the formal surroundings. A jury who had been sitting for the
previous case stayed in their seats, silent,
four-square citizens no doubt feeling equally

244

ill at ease in this unaccustomed role. The coroner, chatting to the clerk, was a large, grey-haired man with a fairly affable demeanour, not forbidding in any way. The clerk gave him some papers, and opened a few windows, and everyone found a seat and the chat faded into silence. It was very warm, in spite of the open windows, and Ros felt a surge of sweat flush beneath her cotton dress as the court waited. Surely it was nervous anticipation? — she was not old enough for the menopause, although at times like this she felt it. She felt plain and depressed and badly in need of a holiday which this year they had unwisely foregone, needing to spend the money on a new bedroom over the garage.

The coroner first called the doctor to give evidence of the cause of death. The bodies of the two boys had been found together on a deserted beach two days after they had disappeared. The river police apparently knew where to look, according to the currents and tides, and at least the parents had been spared the agonies of not having the bodies brought back for what was known as a decent burial. They had died from drowning, the doctor declared, although he used more impressive words, and there were no marks of violence on their bodies.

Tranter and Liz Weston then gave evidence

of identification. Kevin's father gave a tight-lipped and slightly histrionic performance, being stopped by the coroner when he made to add some comments of his own. But to Ros's surprise, Liz was composed and calm, speaking firmly and without nervousness. Ros had supposed giving evidence would be a terrible ordeal for her, but she seemed to take it in her stride. Ros noticed that she was not sitting near Mr Tranter and his lawyer, but on the other side of the court, as far away as she could get. Whether it was coincidental or intended one could not tell.

A police inspector next gave evidence of the finding of the bodies, reading times and places from his notes, practised and stolid. After he had sat down, the coroner spent some time reading his notes, and then nodded to the clerk to call the next witness.

'Miss Penelope Anne Curtis, please.'

Penny came to the witness box and was sworn in. She looked very young, almost a child herself, slender and brown and vulnerable.

The coroner, still half-reading his notes, glanced at her and cleared his throat.

'Now, I understand that you were working with these children when these two boys disappeared off the boat? Can you tell me about it?'

His voice was avuncular, encouraging. He turned away from his notes and looked at Penny over the tops of his gold-rimmed glasses.

'What happened?'

'We were all below, everyone. We had had our dinner and I was washing up. The children were drying and tidying. I wanted a bucket to soak the stew pan in. The galley bucket had crabs in that the children had caught so I asked someone to go and fetch the bucket from on deck. It was kept just outside the hatchway, for swabbing the decks with. Daniel volunteered so I sent him. I think Kevin went with him but at the time I didn't notice. Then almost immediately I saw water gushing out on to the floor from the cupboard under the sink. Stevie was sitting at the table so I asked him to fetch the skipper.'

'Who was where?'

'In his cuddy, with Mrs Monk. He came at once and we were all down on the floor stopping the water, and the children were excited and larking about. I thought it might be serious but it was only the clip come off the hose, nothing at all.'

'But it served as a distraction, I understand?'

'Yes. Yes, it did. There was a lot of water suddenly. But Nick put it right very quickly.

Then Mrs Monk came and told the children to clear out of the galley into the saloon, and I stayed there tidying up and mopping up the floor properly. When I had finished the children were all sitting round the saloon table and I heard Mrs Monk say, 'Who's missing?'

'And that was the first time anyone noticed the two boys were missing?'

'Yes.'

'So how long would that have been since you told Daniel to fetch the bucket?'

'Not long. Perhaps five minutes. I couldn't say exactly. Perhaps a bit more. I told Mrs Monk that I'd sent them to fetch a bucket, and Mrs Monk went on deck to see where they were. I got on with giving out paper and telling the children what we were going to do next, and I didn't give a thought to the other matter until Mrs Monk came back and said they weren't on deck.'

'And that was the last anyone saw of them?'

'Yes, sir.'

The coroner made some notes and there was a long silence while he did so. The members of the Press were all writing busily.

The coroner came out of his papers and said to Penny, 'When the children were on deck did they wear life-jackets?'

'Yes, it was a very strict rule. Always.'

'But we will assume the two boys wouldn't have put life-jackets on just to fetch a bucket?'

'No. Not as the bucket was very close to the companionway. I didn't tell them to, and wouldn't have expected it.'

'Thank you, Miss Curtis. I think you have described the picture quite adequately. The last that was seen of the boys was as they went up the ladder — the companionway — to fetch the bucket?'

'Yes, that's right.'

'You may stand down now.'

'Thank you.'

Looking relieved and near to tears, Penny returned to her seat near Jo and Nick. Ros noticed that Stevie and Norm were sitting whispering together. The jury stared stonily ahead. Tranter's lawyer said something to the doctor, who smiled. For some it was all in a normal day's work, but for others it was the ordeal of a lifetime.

The coroner turned to the clerk and said, 'I think we'll have the skipper next. Nicholas Arthur Melville.'

'Nicholas Arthur Melville, please!'

Nick got up and came down the aisle to the witness stand, looking very clean and stricken, and slightly strange in his borrowed navy-blue suit, a size or two too large for him.

He looked extremely young, Ros noticed, just as Penny had. She knew he was twenty-eight, but he looked more like eighteen. It was the bum life he led, she thought. No responsibilities. Not till now.

'You are the skipper of the sailing barge *Adeline*, are you not?'

'Yes, sir.'

'Can you describe this barge, and tell us how easy it might be to fall overboard? Does it have rails to stop a person falling over the side?'

'No, sir. She has solid bulwarks all round her, but they aren't very high. Only about two foot.'

'No guard lines above?'

'No, sir. No barge has guard-rails.'

'So in fact it would be quite easy to fall overboard?'

'Not when the boat is quiet at anchor, sir, as she was that night. And at any time, a barge is very solid, deliberate like. People don't fall overboard easy.'

'But no one saw what happened to these two boys. As skipper, do you have any ideas of how they came to fall overboard? Do you think they were larking about, fighting perhaps?'

'We have a theory, sir, but no proof that it happened like it.'

'What's your theory?'

'The bucket, sir — we used it for pulling up sea-water to wash down the decks. But the children knew they were forbidden to do this. We made it quite clear. It can be very dangerous if you don't know how, especially when the barge is sailing. When the bucket fills, the weight of the water gives a very strong and sudden tug on the rope, and a child not used to it would most probably lose the bucket, or quite likely be tugged in if he didn't let go quick enough. But the boys were always asking to have a try. It seemed to fascinate them. We think that's perhaps what happened.'

'That one of the boys had a try at filling the bucket, and was pulled in?'

'Yes, sir. I reckon he'd have held on, you see, for fear of losing the bucket, knowing that what he was doing was forbidden. And perhaps the other one went in thinking he could save him. They were both good swimmers, you see, confident, and they wouldn't realise how strong the tide runs. It was top of the ebb at the time, running its fastest. And the bucket was missing. We never found the bucket.'

'Hmm.'

A long contemplative silence while the coroner stared at his notes.

'Thank you, Mr Melville. I think that's all I need to ask you. You may stand down.'

Nick retreated, and Norm was called, to reiterate how the two boys had asked to be allowed to fill the bucket over the side and how he had forbidden them.

Next came Stevie. As he took the witness box there was a marked stir of interest in the Press benches, and even the jury perked up and smiled at each other. Stevie had not changed into a suit for the occasion, but was in the ubiquitous skin-tight jeans and black leather jacket, his quiff the usual bright pink. Ros, seeing him now as others saw him, and not as the accepted furniture of her classroom, wondered whether he was going to do the cause a lot of good. During the six months or so that he had been in her classroom, she had never actually had a conversation with him, nor had anyone else in the school as far as she knew. He never spoke except to the children, apart from a few necessary requests or answers to direct questions; it occurred to Ros that she had no idea how bright he was, or otherwise. Was his remarkable empathy with children a result of his own simple mind? She had always rather assumed that his coming to school was merely a slightly better option than staying in bed in an empty house all day or watching the television. He obviously enjoyed it. He appeared to have no ambition at all. But now, seeing the situation from outside, Ros realised that it was — as Cris Grott had complained from the start — rather odd.

The coroner, not unexpectedly, had some difficulty pinning down Stevie's role.

'You were one of the helpers during the week? Were you part of the crew?'

'No.'

'You're not a schoolteacher?'

'No.'

'What was your role exactly?'

Stevie gave this some thought. 'Just a helper, like.'

'Who asked you to come?'

'Mrs Monk.'

'Oh.'

Another long pause for note-writing.

'I understand you were in the — er — saloon, when Miss Curtis was washing up with the children? What were you doing?'

Stevie groped into his mind, slowly.

'Talking.'

'Who to?'

'Norm.'

'Then what happened?'

'Er . . . Miss shouted to us. The water was spouting out like.'

'She asked you to fetch the skipper?'

'Yes.'

'And you went through to the skipper's quarters where he was talking to Mrs Monk?'

'Yes.'

'And they both came through to see what the matter was?'

'Yes.'

'And during this time did you see the two children, Daniel and Kevin?'

'No.'

'You didn't go up on deck at all?'

'No.'

'Thank you.'

The coroner decided he had had enough of the monasyllabic Stevie and asked him to stand down.

'I think we all have a very fair picture of how this tragic — er — event took place. The last witness I shall call is Mrs Monk, the headmistress. Will you call Mrs Monk, please?'

Jo came firmly to the witness box, looking as impressive as Stevie had looked bizarre. Watching her, Ros felt a sentimental pang of loyalty and affection, and a blur of tears fuzzed her vision. This was where the can-carrying stopped, why she was called last, why Ros had never wanted to be a headmistress. In the end, like the skipper of a boat, everything that happened along the way was ultimately your responsibility, even if you weren't actually present at the time. The accolades, or the sack, came to you.

'Now you will agree, Mrs Monk, that the boys' disappearance took place as described by the other witnesses? Have you anything to add to what has been said?'

'I think the situation has been described very accurately. Everyone was relaxed at the end of a very successful three days aboard the barge, and at exactly the same time as the two boys went up on deck to fetch the bucket there was a distraction below that took everyone's mind off anything else. Although the water gushing into the galley looked rather serious and caused alarm for a few moments, it was actually caused by something very minor. But naturally there was a lot of clearing up to do and quite a bit of excitement, and that was why the boys' disappearance wasn't noticed immediately.'

'How long would you say?'

'I would say something between five and ten minutes.'

'And when you discovered they were missing you instituted a search?'

'Not at once. I went up on deck expecting to find them there. It was a still, fine night. There was no one on deck. I walked from end to end and I looked down the river but could

255

see nothing, no disturbance or anything. I noticed the bucket was missing. I knew then that they must have gone overboard.'

'Did you then send for assistance?'

'The skipper called for assistance on the radio, yes.'

'How long was it coming?'

'The first help, an inflatable with an outboard, arrived within about half an hour. Then other help came, more and more. A helicopter eventually.'

Her voice dropped.

The coroner said gently, 'It must have been a terrible moment for you. Up to then, you had had no safety problems?'

'No. None at all. The children had been well drilled about procedures aboard, wearing life-jackets on deck, how to get into the tender, all that sort of thing. We had had no anxieties at all.'

'When you first had the idea for the expedition, was the question of safety raised?'

'It was discussed at a governors' meeting, yes. And I gave full details to the Education Committee as a matter of course. I myself did not consider it a dangerous undertaking.'

'The parents all gave written permissions? Was it suggested to them that there was any element of danger?'

'Only in so much as there is an element of

danger inevitably if children go near deep water, just as there is when they cross the road in busy traffic. The trip was oversubscribed by three or four times. I had intended to repeat it for the ones who couldn't be fitted in on the first trip.'

'And you had satisfied yourself with the expertise of the skipper and crew of the barge and their suitability for such a trip?'

'Yes. I have known the skipper for a very long time and he is extremely capable. The barge has been refitted recently and has her proper Board of Trade certificate for taking passengers.'

'And so everything was done on this trip that possibly could be done to ensure safety?'

'Yes, in my opinion it was.'

'Thank you very much, Mrs Monk. I don't think there is any more I want to ask you.'

Jo went back to her seat beside Tom and as the coroner paused to say something to the clerk, a small murmuring arose in the court. Ros considered that Jo had come across very intelligently and she felt optimistic for the outcome. Nothing had arisen to suggest that the accident was any more than extraordinarily bad luck, which was the truth. Thank God it was nearly over.

Tranter's lawyer then got up and said something to the coroner. They had a whispered conference, and the coroner said something to the clerk. The court fell silent again and the clerk said, 'Could Mr Steven Arnott just come back to the witness box again, please?'

Stevie got up and stalked back to the witness stand.

Tranter's lawyer said to the coroner, 'With your permission, sir, may I just put one more question to this witness?'

The coroner nodded.

The lawyer said, 'When you went to the skipper's quarters to ask his help, when the water flooded out on the floor, what were Mrs Monk and Mr Melville doing?'

'They were kissing. Kissing and drinking gin.'

At this remarkable reply there was a collected gasp of surprise across the courtroom. The Press buzzed with satisfaction, and scribbled madly.

The lawyer said, 'Thank you, Mr Arnott. That's all.'

The coroner looked confused. He waited until Stevie had sat down and said, 'Mrs Monk, do you want to say anything? You needn't if you don't want to. But you have an opportunity. You can speak from where you're sitting.'

Jo stood up. 'When Stevie came in, I had

just kissed Nick on the cheek. The trip had been very successful and I was very happy. I've known Nick since we were at school together. I felt relaxed and very pleased at the way the expedition had gone and that was why I kissed him.'

She sat down and a hubbub of conversation rose in the court, the mood quite definitely changed from hushed sympathy to bright inquisitiveness. Tranter's lawyer looked indifferent, but Tranter looked extremely pleased with himself. Ros, feeling that she had received a blow to the jaw, saw Ann Forrester say something to Cris in the row in front of her, and the same spark of pleasure was in her face. Ros now knew what Stevie had been doing in Cris's house. Her spying through the geraniums should have prepared her for something like this, but she had never suspected the worst of human nature, found it hard to believe that Cris and Ann Forrester and Tranter between them could use such a despicable method to put Jo in a bad light. That this was why the question had been put to Stevie Ros was convinced. Whatever Jo might have said to excuse herself, nothing was going to detract from Stevie's blunt shock to the court: 'They were kissing and drinking gin.'

The jury filed out to consider their verdict.

The court broke into eager chat and quite a lot of the pressmen hurried out. Ros, unable to contain her resentment, bent forward and said to Crispin, 'I saw Stevie in your house last night. I can see why you suddenly decided to be friends with him now, Cris. I think your behaviour is absolutely despicable.'

Crispin turned an unbecoming shade of beetroot.

Ann Forrester turned aggressively to Ros. 'The whole truth should be told. That is what this enquiry is for. Are you suggesting Stevie lied?'

'No. But the way he put it was incriminating and meant to be incriminating. And I suggest you put him up to it, probably with Mr Tranter's help. I wouldn't even be surprised if you bribed him.'

Ros could fast feel herself losing her temper, and knew it wasn't the time and place. Ann never let an argument go, as Ros well knew. Her beady eyes were bright with vicious enjoyment.

'You are close to being slanderous, Mrs Taylor. Stevie only stated the truth. Why should he wish to harm Mrs Monk when she has been so kind to him? If she trusts him, surely we all can?'

Very snide, very vicious.

'What's more, Mrs Taylor, why did Mrs

Monk choose to charter that particular barge when there are half a dozen barges with more chartering experience than Mr Melville's? We all know that Mr Monk is looking elsewhere for female companionship, after all. It is not unreasonable to assume that his wife needs comfort in such a situation.'

'I beg your pardon?' Ros's head reeled.

'I know that he spent the night with another woman in a hotel in Newmarket quite recently. Of course it is no concern of mine. But I suggest that there are very good reasons why it might be assumed that Mrs Monk is not entirely emotionally sound at the moment.'

Ros was literally speechless. Her mouth dropped open.

'You may accuse me, as a governor, of not being supportive, but my duty is to the school, not merely to its head. Some of us can see through Mrs Monk's charm, and it is the children's interests that are paramount.'

She would have found something even more outrageous to say, no doubt, if the jury had not at this point started to come back into the courtroom. Ros could scarcely believe the woman's vituperation.

'You cow!' she cried out.

The courtroom having quietened at the jury's reappearance, her voice did not go altogether unheard. There was a shocked rustle and some tittering, and Ros leapt to her feet and fled. Outside the door she stood shaking with rage. However it went now, Jo would be branded by that evil woman's manipulation of stupid Stevie with his 'kissing and drinking gin'. Ros could see the reporters buzzing round the telephone booths in the hall below, galvanised from their seats by the whiff of scandal. It would not matter one jot that Jo was cleared and innocent of being in any way careless and irresponsible in looking after the children, not if she could be tagged with immorality in the same breath. All newspapers wanted a story and there were no stories in being hardworking, responsible and above reproach. Had Tom really been unfaithful? Ros went slowly down the stairs, remembering her own thoughts on the subject earlier, when Jo had told her of their irreconcilable argument about having a baby. In a way, Jo's refusal could be considered a negation of the marriage partnership and perhaps after that final and bitter argument Tom had considered himself free to look elsewhere. Why not indeed? Ros knew that her own marriage and home would never withstand her being a headmistress. She was stretching it to its limits as it was, trying to do her best by all and mostly failing, getting by on compromise. Lucky Dave was easy-going — even his concert shirts went unironed quite often but he rarely complained. No wonder she left the rails when confronted by such as Ann Forrester, whose time was wholly free for making mischief.

Downstairs another group of people were waiting outside the door of Court Three in exactly the same state of nervous anticipation as Ros had witnessed amongst her own friends earlier. The shuffle inside showed that the hearing had ended. Ros stood waiting for Jo, jostled by the reporters who were coming back like migrating starlings. One of them grabbed her arm.

'I understand you're a teacher at the same school? Can you tell me — '

'Oh, for God's sake!' Ros snatched her arm away.

'Is that pink-haired geezer actually a teacher?'

'Of course not!'

'What's his place in the picture then? It wasn't clear.'

'He — he — '

The reporter was poised like a vulture.

'He's the brother of a pupil. Went along to help. Knows the children, they like him.'

'Mrs Monk likes him?'

'I beg your pardon?'

'Mrs Monk — I understand her marriage is breaking up?'

'What are you saying?'

'Her husband's got another woman. Do you know about this?'

'Where do you get this rubbish from? Look, that's her husband holding her arm over there.'

Ros flounced away, making for Tom and Jo.

Tom saw her and said, 'Let's get out of here. This is no place to stand chatting, not with this mob.'

With his arm round Jo he steered her firmly away towards the staircase. Ros followed. Outside the door photographers jostled and called out. Stevie was standing on the steps with light-bulbs popping all round him, grinning happily. But when Jo appeared the light-bulbs all flashed in her direction and for a few moments their way was completely barred. Questions rained from all sides.

Tom said to Jo, 'Don't look uptight. Look cheerful. There's no need to say a thing, but it doesn't pay to get cross.'

'They're only doing their job, I'm sure,' Jo said savagely.

She smiled into the cameras.

Tranter was coming out with his lawyer.

'Mr Tranter, are you satisfied with the verdict?' someone called out.

Tom and Jo plunged on down the steps and Ros followed, appalled.

'Let them talk to him. He'll tell them a few stories,' Jo said.

'What was the verdict? I had such a row with Ann Forrester up in the gallery I had to leave the court before the jury came back.' Ros glanced round and was relieved to see that the pack, having got their pictures of Jo, were no longer following. They were clustered round Tranter.

'Death by Misadventure. She was absolutely cleared as we knew she would be,' Tom said tersely. 'Apart from Stevie's nonsense, it couldn't have gone better.'

'Stevie's nonsense was the only interesting bit, the rest was so boringly true,' Jo snapped. 'What do you think will be in the newspapers tomorrow? The interesting bit, naturally.'

'Look, do you want to go home or shall we all go for a slap-up meal?' Tom asked.

'Or a bottle of gin?'

'Oh, shut up, Jo. A good lunch? What do you think, Ros?'

'I think we've deserved one, yes. And a large gin for Jo, why not?'

'Drink to dear Stevie. I was the one that trusted him, of them all. How stupid can you get? I should have listened to Grott. Grott was right all along. Hats off to Grott. I should have kicked Stevie out and never gone on the dangerous water, and everything would have been all right.'

'Have you quite finished, dearest?' Tom asked heavily.

'Oh, yes, probably. It's true that a strong gin would be very desirable at the moment.'

'We'd better get drunk where the press won't see us, in that case.'

'Not to mention the governors and the members of the Education Committee.'

They tumbled into the car and Tom drove away out of town. Jo then remembered Penny and Nick and Norm — 'I never thanked them, I never spoke to them. Penny might have needed a lift.'

'She went with Nick, I saw her,' Ros said. 'Stop worrying.'

'Penny was great. So was Nick.'

'But not Stevie.'

'Not Stevie.' Jo started to laugh. 'My God, whatever did they make of him? There is a funny side to it, if you look hard enough.'

Ros did not think it would be politic to say what she had seen through the geraniums. Not today. Later perhaps. Jo was in a strange, slightly hysterical mood. Tom took them a long way away to an ancient Tudor road-house with gardens that ran down to a clear-running stream. He sat them kindly on the bank and said he would fetch them gin, on a tray, and the menu.

'Lie in the sun, girls, and relax.'

'He is so clever, your Tom,' Ros said when he had departed. The stream was entirely therapeutic, small fish gliding in transparent pools, the sun sparking and spearing delightfully through softly-waving rushes.

'Not my Tom any more,' Jo said. 'Somebody else's Tom.'

'I find that hard to believe.'

They lay curled on the grass, watching the fish.

'It doesn't matter, actually. Nothing really matters any more. Like this business today, things are out of your hands, you're not in control any more. One just has to get accustomed to it. It's never happened to me before.'

'It's most people's lot, all the time. Mine, for example. Hanging on. I haven't felt totally in control of anything for years. Your standards are too high, Jo. Relax.'

'Mm. I might have to. Get fat and lazy.' She smiled.

'It might suit you.'

'Not the way Tom wants though.'

'Is the somebody else going to give him what he wants? Is that why?'

'I think so. We haven't really discussed it, to tell you the truth. I only found out on our way home from Scotland. I hadn't noticed anything different, which shows how little attention I spare for him in the normal course of events. Only when I found out I remembered all sorts of clues — if only I had been interested enough to pick them up. I haven't been much of a wife to him, I suppose.'

'Oh, lor', roll on the violins! He'll be lucky if he finds another half as good! It's not like you to be so wimpish, Jo. If you want him you'll have to fight for him — if not, get on with being a career woman. It'll all come right sooner or later.'

'It'll come wrong tomorrow, when we see the papers!'

Tom was coming back with the drinks and the menu. He set them down on the grass and they concentrated their demoralised minds on the task of choosing a bracing lunch. Tom, for an erring husband, was uncommonly tactful to Jo. Ros, not for the first time, found herself thinking what a jewel he was, as husbands went. Most women would be only too pleased to bear a replica. Jo's phobia against child-bearing was incomprehensible to Ros.

'Boeuf Bourguignonne,' said Tom.

'Hell, it's not a Boeuf Bourguignonne day!' said Jo.

'Speak for yourself.'

'Melon for starters.'

'Taramasalata,' said Ros.

They lay in the grass, concentrating on distraction. The horrors of tomorrow's newspapers hung over them, inescapable like the hum of traffic on the road beyond the stream. Stevie's photograph, grinning, captioned — probably — as one of the teachers, was going to do the cause no good at all, apart from his stunning indictment of Jo's behaviour.

Over the meal, Tom was quiet. He could not stop his mind going to Camilla. He had tried to put his anxieties on her account out of his mind while sorting out Jo's problems, but he could ignore her disappearance no longer. She must be found. The longer she was missing, the more likely it seemed that she might have . . . he found it hard to admit, to put into words, that a woman might commit suicide on his account. It seemed an incredibly vain thought. But she was an acknowledged loner, without friends or hope, of a depressive turn of mind. Her complete disappearance was disturbing.

While Jo and Ros talked over coffee, Tom excused himself and went out to the telephone. He rang Camilla's aunt in London, and discovered that no word had come as to her whereabouts, or even existence.

'I've told her mum and dad she seems to have gone missing. I've rung her work place but they're in the dark too. I really don't know what can have become of her. I'm really worried. I've even told the police, but they didn't seem very interested. Took her description, like, but I've never heard back from them.'

Tom made a few platitudinous comforting remarks and rang off. He went back to the two women.

'Are you done? Shall we go?'

He paid the bill. They went back to the car, Jo and Ros talking shop in a way that excluded him completely. He decided suddenly that he had neglected Camilla's disappearance in deference to Jo's business for far too long. There was no more he could do for Jo, but everything for Camilla.

'I'll drop you at home and then I think I'll go up to the office. See what's been happening while I've been away,' he said to Jo.

'I thought perhaps I should go and see Liz Weston,' Jo said, unexpectedly. 'Now it's all over . . . explain a bit. Tell her that what

Stevie said wasn't true — at least, not in the way he made it sound. I don't care about anyone else — what they think — but I care very much that she knows what's true and what isn't.'

'Okay. Good idea.'

If Jo thought there was an ulterior motive in his going to London, she did not mention it. Ros was delivered back to her large pile of ironing, Jo to Liz Weston's house, and Tom drove away.

Liz's neighbour said Liz had gone for a walk on the seawall.

'She said she wanted to think about things. I worry about her, you know. She's a funny woman.'

'She's had a tough time.'

Liz's neighbour paid lip service to sympathy, but had been remarkably unhelpful in fact. It was the stalwart tweeds-and-brogues ladies who ran the Over-Sixties Club that had briskly taken Liz in hand. Perhaps the seawall was a refuge from their bracing support.

Jo walked out beside the tidal ditch towards the seawall. Alone now, she felt shaken, in disarray. The inquest had not cleared up the case, only made her own situation a lot worse. She was more or less on a par with Liz now, without prospects or hope. She felt Tom had gone from her, and now it seemed likely

271

her job had gone as well. All the rage and indignation had died. As she walked through the long grass, the tide lapping on the stones below, the hot sun on her back, she felt somehow simplified, her cause lost, the turmoil over. It might be defeat, but suddenly it seemed very peaceful.

Liz was sitting on the wall a mile down. She looked startled at Jo's appearance.

'I wanted to talk to you.'

'What about?'

'I'm sorry, that's all really. And what Stevie said wasn't true. Not like he made it sound.'

'I know.'

'I loved Daniel. He was the best.'

Jo sat down.

Liz said, 'Mr Tranter tried to make me go in with him, with the lawyer and everything, against you. He got that Mrs Forrester on his side, and Mr Grott. They got Stevie to say that, I think.'

'Yes, Ros — Mrs Taylor — told me. He wasn't really lying. I did give Nick a kiss, out of happiness, and the gin — that was rubbish, it was nearly all tonic water. But he spoke the truth, I suppose. I just wanted you to know, so that when the papers come tomorrow, you won't think too badly of me.'

'I don't. I never have.'

'You've every reason.'

'No. I don't think like that. I wanted him to go on the trip. I bet he loved it.'

'Yes, he did. He was splendid.'

'It's different now. I never got over Pete. And now this with Daniel, I seem to have come through. I thought at first I would die, but somehow I feel very peaceful now, it's very strange. I feel I've had a lot given to me. It's been taken away too, but I've had it. And now I'm on my own again, I feel ready to start my own life afresh. I've absolutely nothing to lose any more. A clean slate. And instead of being frightened, I feel quite excited. It's very strange.'

Jo wondered if she was on tranquilisers, and decided not. She wouldn't have the doctor, Jo remembered Dave saying that. Jo wondered, when she got over this herself, whether she would feel the same. She was about to lose everything too. But her slate was not clean at all. Not at the moment.

They sat watching the tide sliding out of the creek, uncovering the silver mud and all the goodies for the sandpipers and dunlins that twitted and dipped on the water's edge. Apart from the birds, it was silent. There was no wind. Neither of them said any more.

★　★　★

And Tom, after he had visited his own office and Camilla's office and haunted Covent Garden for a haphazard hour, landed up in his lunch-hour church where once Camilla had sung in the choir and, sitting in a pew, reviewed the state of his life in similar fashion. It was a mess.

Nobody had heard of Camilla. But Camilla was all he wanted.

He sat in the slanting late afternoon rays of sunshine that somehow managed to squeeze between high office blocks to infiltrate the hidden church and wondered how he had managed to come to such a pass. Even with the shock of Jo's accident, he could have arranged things better when he parted from Camilla. He had behaved brutally towards her, without thinking. Promised her the moon, and vanished.

The last of the rush-hour traffic swirled around his small oasis, its roar muffled by close-fitting doors and thick stone walls. If he sat long enough she might come, he thought. And knew she wouldn't. Whatever Jo decided now, that marriage was doomed. He could no longer make love to her; the act had been a parody for some time already, and every day she slipped farther and farther away from him. Their old companionship was not enough. So from having two women to love, which had made him feel so rich and bewildered, he now had none at all, and no prospects. So much for the perpetuation of the Monkhood.

He went on sitting there until the sun had gone. The church became cool and mysterious, a vaccuum of past sorrows, for ever now obscured. Tom's present grief was a mere speck in history, its breath scarcely disturbing the rich gauze of the church's experience through centuries. Who was Camilla, or indeed himself, to expect the church to heed, although they had loved it and found solace there? Tom did not believe in prayer or religion, although he used this church. He used it rather like a club, for somewhere to sit, to think.

When he got home it was late and Jo was already in bed. He got in beside her.

'Did you see Camilla?'

'No.'

'You really went to the office?'

'Yes. I would like to have seen Camilla, if that's what you mean. But she's vanished. Nobody knows where she is.'

'Oh.' After a pause, 'Poor you.'

There seemed no more to be said, on either side. Tom felt that they had already decided to follow their own paths, without discussion. Jo was totally immersed in her own problems, as he was now with his. What a dull ending to a dull marriage, not with a bang, not even with a whimper. Tom, who knew he was dull, nevertheless felt hopelessly disappointed.

In the morning he drove out to collect all the newspapers.

They were mostly divided as to whether to splash the front page with a picture of Jo, headed 'Kissing and Drinking', or Stevie headed, variously, 'Teacher Tells Tales', 'Tales out of School' or 'Teacher Alleges Kissing and Drinking'. They nearly all called Stevie a teacher or, at best, teacher's assistant. The small print was fairly accurate, and the verdict of Death by Misadventure correctly given, but the overall picture was luridly coloured by the one small phrase elicited by Tranter's solicitor. Most papers said that Mr Tranter intended to take the case further. In all it was front page news.

Jo, having expected the worst, found she had no more emotion left to be stirred. She had a violent headache, and a temper to match. Tom went to the office and immersed himself in catching up on work. When he got home he found Jo slumped in the armchair, looking like a shadow of her usual self.

'I've got the sack,' she said.

Tom did not find this altogether a great surprise.

'They call it something else of course, 'temporary suspension' — full pay, my dear, just while we sort things out.'

'It's very hard for them, given what all your parents have been reading in the papers today,' Tom said mildly.

'I think they should have stood by me.'

'Yes. But very tricky for them. People like Tranter, for instance . . . '

'They said they've had a lot of what they call adverse reaction on the phone, parents sounding off, outraged. And as term is due to start next week, they suggest I stand down until the matter is given a full discussion. In effect it means they believe Stevie.'

'Have you heard from the governors?'

'Yes, very sympathetic. Full support — presumably excepting Ann Forrester, although he didn't say so. But of course they don't count for anything when it comes to the nitty-gritty.'

'But what about the school? Without you — ?'

'Grott is going to be appointed Acting Head, for the time being.'

'Oh God! Why not Ros? She's Deputy.'

'She won't do it. I've begged and pleaded, but no, she won't. More than her marriage is worth, she says. Even for me. So it's all finished, all I've worked for, all I've done.'

'That's not true. You take it too seriously.'

'No. It is serious, or not worth doing. I'm going to resign and bugger off. They can keep their bloody salary. I'm not going to be kept on a shelf till it suits them to move me sideways somewhere.'

'Sit on it for a few days. Things will settle down.'

'No.'

She was like that, after all. Always had been.

'It's ironic,' he said, 'you doing so much extra for the sake of the children, and this is where it gets you. And they get Grott instead. I wonder if he'll get rid of Stevie? Considering he owes the job to him. A ticklish little problem for him, before he even starts.'

'He won't be able to cope, I know that.'

Tom could see a bleak evening ahead. Outside it was balmy and warm, and the cows grazed peacefully up on the hill behind the church. He thought fleetingly of Camilla and the hillside above the Bed and Breakfast, the cows coming down the lane. A twist of pain for the gap where she had been sickened him. He knew that Jo had no use for him, even in her present extremity; he was only a companion, no more. He had no intention of asking her again, but, as if she

278

knew, she said angrily,

'And no, I won't have your bloody baby either.'

Then she was sorry. 'I don't mean to shout it out. But this doesn't change anything on that score. Don't get any ideas.'

'No.'

There really was nothing left between them, suddenly.

But strangely, perhaps because they both now knew exactly how things were, after a long period of doubt, the evening passed peacefully in unrancourous conversation and reminiscences, the companionable fixing of a meal, watching a good programme on the television.

The next morning Jo packed her bags and went out to her car.

'I'm going up to Betty's,' she said. 'You'll hear from me.'

She kissed him without emotion. 'Thanks,' she said.

When her car was out of sight Tom wondered, 'Thanks for what?' A marriage? Did a marriage truly end so simply? Perhaps he was lucky, rather than otherwise.

He went back to work. There was nothing else to do, after all.

# 9

It was some three or four weeks later that Tom thought of the Battersea Dogs Home. Camilla had gone there in distress after the break-up of her last affair. Could she possibly have called a second time? It was a remote, pathetic chance, but Tom was clutching at straws. He was beginning to accept that she was dead or, if not, had started a new life somewhere away from anyone she knew. He found a photo of her, and called one evening after work. He felt an idiot, rubbing shoulders with people who had come to look for their lost dog, not their lost girlfriend. The girl he spoke to thought it rather funny too.

'She's not been brought in, no.' She giggled.

Tom was not very amused. 'She chose a dog from here once, not all that long ago. It got run over and I wondered if she had called again. You might have her address?'

Perhaps he looked as pathetic as some of the inmates, for the girl sobered up and said she would 'ask around'.

'Not everybody's here just now. If you leave it, and anyone remembers, I'll give you a ring, if you like. If you leave a number.'

Tom left his office number, and his home number. He forgot all about it. He had dropped into a boring, hard-working existence, almost as if his life hadn't been disrupted at all. He had a woman in to clean the house and get some shopping for him; he ate frozen food and took his own suits to be cleaned. Sometimes Ros came to see him. She said Liz Weston had started a teacher-training course, and Grott was hopeless. The school was going to the dogs. 'I think I'm going to leave.'

Tom discovered he wasn't interested.

'Poor old Tom,' said Ros tenderly. 'Have you heard from Jo?'

'Yes, she keeps in touch. She's got a job in Edinburgh.'

'Yes, she wrote to me too. ESN teaching. She loves it.'

'She would.'

But there was no bitterness. Tom was still fond of Jo, but did not miss her very much. It was a quite a surprise to find out how little passion there had been between them, more a civilised friendship and, even then, without much common ground.

'As long as she hasn't gone out of teaching, it really doesn't matter,' Ros said. 'Our loss is their gain. Good luck to them.'

When he had quite forgotten about Battersea Dogs Home, he got a phone call at his office.

'About this girlfriend of yours . . . ' It took him some time to cotton on.

'It's Battersea Dogs Home.'

'Christ!' Of course! Sick, giddy excitement flooded him. 'What is it?'

'Well, this girl . . . there's someone here who thinks it's someone who came for a dog, to give a dog a home. There was a terrific argument — she wanted one that somebody else wanted — that's why they remember her. Perhaps if you can call round, you can talk to the girl who thinks it's her. Eileen she's called. She says it's the same as the photograph.'

'Did she leave an address?'

'Well, no, but the other person did, the person who got the dog.'

'I don't follow.'

'No, it's awfully complicated. Can you call round some time?'

'I'll come, yes. I'll come at once.'

He fled out into the street and hailed a taxi. As he sat there, fuming at red lights and blocked streets, he realised that his adrenalin was running, his heart thumping, as if he were a mere youth going to a first date. The life that had become so dreary of late, his passionless parting from Jo, was now revealed as symptoms of a condition: he was quite definitely in love, and suffering from separation from the beloved. Lovesick! The very thought now of seeing Camilla again was causing a classic fever of the brain. For some reason he had thought his preoccupation with her where-abouts was a sort of duty, compounded of guilt, but now he knew that all the time he had been suffering from the oldest sickness in the world. The greyness of his present existence broke into a thousand Beano-esque stars and Pows! and Whams! as he shivered in the back of the taxi. Battersea Dogs Home! What a tryst for a lover!

The noise, the smell . . . 'Eileen? Oh, I'll see if I can find her? Wait here, will you?' . . . Camilla! He could not sit still, but had to pace about in the office, buffeted by comings and goings and phone calls and the eternal barking.

'I'm Eileen. Are you the man about the girl in the photo?'

She was plump and cheerful, smelling of disinfectant.

'Well, I think it was the same woman. I never got her name — she never gave it, because there was this argument, you see.'

'No.'

'She said she wanted a dog. She looked

around and chose one, not knowing that this other guy had just said he wanted it. It was a white bull terrier called Smiler. I mean, of all the dogs in here, we had these two people both wanting the same dog at the same moment, and neither of them were prepared to give way. This guy, he'd just told Maureen it was the one he wanted, and she went to get a lead and he wandered off somewhere for a minute, and when Maureen got back there was this woman saying she had chosen Smiler. And Maureen said about Smiler had just been picked by someone else, and she got all neurotic and peculiar and said it was Smiler or nothing. And the guy came back and he wasn't going to give way either. It was really odd, they were a couple of weirdos. And then the guy said to this woman, 'We'll both take the dog, and we'll go and settle it over a drink, how about that?' And Maureen said they couldn't both have the dog, it would have to be one or the other, officially — you have to pay for them, of course, and who was going to pay? — so they got quite sensible after that, and it was sorted out. The man had the dog, officially, but they went off together like old pals, to have a drink. And I'm pretty sure this woman was the same as your photo.'

She pulled the photo out of her pocket and gave it back to him.

'Her.'

'And you got her address? She gave you an address?'

'No. Only the guy's address.'

'Can you give me the guy's address?'

'Well, yes, I suppose so. It'll be in the files somewhere.'

'Can you find it for me? I — I'll make a contribution — pay you for the trouble.'

'Well, not me. The Home, if you like.'

'Yes, of course. Anything. Please.'

He felt quite desperate. It was the only clue he had had since he had parted from Camilla weeks ago. It was ominous in the extreme . . . going off with a total stranger. Was she really that lonely?

'What was he like, this man?'

'I was in the office. You ought to ask Maureen really. She doesn't think it's the same woman, but I do. I saw her when they came back to the office with Smiler. The man was youngish, jeans, leather jacket, sounded Australian to me. He said he ran every morning, round Kensington Gardens or somewhere, and it was boring, and he thought it would be nice for a dog. He'd always had a dog, missed having a dog. He liked bull terriers.'

'Why couldn't she choose another dog? What was so special about Smiler?'

'Oh, Smiler was one of those dogs that could look really pathetic. You know those long, turned-down noses they have? And he had a way of sitting with his back legs sticking out at the side, and looking at you as if he was out in the cold. He could look a real tear-jerker dog. I suppose she just fell for him. People do, you know.'

She fell for me, Tom wanted to say. But she'd gone off with an Aussie.

Eileen found the man's name and address for him, and he put a twenty pound note in the collecting box.

He went outside, clutching his bit of paper. Rod Bellingham, it said. The address was far from slummy, a road of Victorian buildings, now flats, behind the Albert Hall. Tom got another taxi there. He felt he was moving like a puppet, moving by numbers, his mind a blank. He was scared to think anything was going to come of this scrap of paper. Scared of Rod Bellingham, an athletic young Aussie in jeans who presumably liked the look of Camilla enough to ask her out for a drink. What if she was now living with him and Smiler behind the Albert Hall? Very handy for concerts. A lonely woman could easily take up with Rod Bellingham. As the taxi neared Knightsbridge, Rod Bellingham became more and more appealing in Tom's imagination.

Homesick — he wanted a dog — and romantic, wide open to taking a lover. He and Camilla were made for each other, joined by Smiler.

He was dropped outside the block of flats. He found the name on the list beside the door, and pressed the buzzer for the entryphone. No reply. No distant barking.

He stood, feeling cold and stoned. There was a sniff of autumn in the soft, grey afternoon. Tom walked up to Knightsbridge and looked across towards the park railings opposite. People walked mistily beneath the yellowing trees, and dogs that were not Smiler trailed them across the grass. Tom didn't know what to do. He could not leave his place without contacting Rod Bellingham. Even now he might be quite close to Camilla. She might have just gone out, with the dog, to get Rod's shopping, a couple of chops perhaps, and some vegetables. Tom it was who felt lonely now. If nothing came of this he would have to get himself a dog too. He decided he wanted a drink, but it was too early. A meal. He wandered off towards Kensington High Street, steeped in self-pity.

Two hours later he went back to Rod Bellingham's flat. This time a tinny voice answered his bell.

'Yeah? Who is it?'

'Rod Bellingham?'

'Yeah.'

'You don't know me. My name's Tom Monk. Can I have a word with you? Five minutes?'

'Come up.'

The door was released and Tom went two at a time up the stairs to the top of the building. He was still fit, he noticed in passing, and had plenty of breath left by the time he got to Rod's door. It was open. Tom knocked and peered in.

'Rod?'

'Hi, mate, come in.'

Rod was alone in a large untidy bedsitter. Tom felt an immediate calm descend on him, like blanket fog. No Camilla. He stood dully, feeling rather foolish.

'Sorry to butt in on you. I'm looking for someone called Camilla Hastings, and I was given your name and address. It might be a mistake, of course.'

Rod grinned. He was disarmingly young, and definitely attractive, not seedy at all. He looked clean-cut and honest and reliable.

'She was a mistake. Yes, you can say that again. Want a beer?'

Tom felt his buoyancy return with a palpable rush. Hot, sticky excitement — 'Yes, great!' He tried to sound unconcerned.

'Where is she?'

'Gawd knows, mate. Lager or bitter?'

'Bitter, please. You don't know?'

'Buggered off, took the bloody dog with her. You knew about the dog?'

'Yes, I heard about the dog.'

Rod threw him a can of beer out of the fridge.

'That's all I know, mate. She stayed one night, slept with all her clothes on — had the dog in with her — next day after I'd gone to work, that was it. Scarpered. Dog and all.'

'Where to?'

'Search me. If I knew I'd go and get the dog. It was a nice dog.'

Tom showed Rod the photo. 'It was her?'

'That's her. No mistake. Camilla, she said her name was.'

'Oh, Christ!'

Tom's expectations, disappointments and fears had had his emotions going like a yoyo. He now sank down with his beer feeling sick and tired. At least he knew she was still alive. He ought to feel relieved and optimistic, but he didn't. He felt very much like getting drunk.

Rod was not averse to the idea. He said he knew of a good place in Earl's Court, meet a few mates, Tom would like them. Tom didn't care. They went out and got a taxi and Tom got drunk in Earl's Court. Before he was too far gone, he thought to go home and phone Camilla's aunt. He thought Camilla might have gone back there.

'I haven't heard a word, no.'

'Well, she's alive and in London, at least she was recently. I've met people who've seen her. It's definitely her.'

The aunt, instead of being grateful for the news, was outraged.

'And me worried sick all this time!'

Her tirade made Tom see only too clearly what Camilla wanted to escape from. How wise of Camilla, having broken away, to leave the gap unclosed. Tom put the phone down while the castigation continued, and went back with relief to his carefree Aussie companions. A few more drinks and he no longer knew what he thought at all.

He slept the remainder of the night in Rod's flat, on a sagging divan where presumably Camilla had slept with the dog.

When he awoke, it was to the rattle of milk bottles in the street below. It was still early, but light. Strangely, London was quieter than his country home, where one was awoken by the lowing of cows, the din of cocks, ducks and tractors and — if one were unaccustomed — the church clock as well. Here there was a muted murmur of traffic far away, the homely milkman, a pattern of softly moving shadows on the ceiling from a plane tree outside, soothing to the turgid brain. Tom opened his eyes wider and looked around.

The room, although large enough and relatively pleasant, had the same hung-over air as its two occupants. It smelled of beer, and the floor was strewn with their clothes as they had stumbled out of them the night before. Two dirty saucepans stood on the miniature cooker in one corner and there was a stack of used plates and teamugs in the sink. The rubbish bin needed emptying. There was a damp stain on the ceiling over his head, and the very old wallpaper bulged, even very gently waved, in the draught through the top of the long sash-window. The room had the time-honoured smell of nearly all male-inhabited bedsits: of old socks and old food; it brought back strongly Tom's memories of student days; he went in those few moments back ten years or more, even to the headache. He lay taking it all in, and thought of Camilla lying there on just this same lumpy divan taking it in in just the same way. The ten unrewarding years with Jake must have flooded back — she had once recalled the smell of his feet and underpants with distaste, describing the life to Tom; she too must have taken in the stains on the

291

ceiling and washing-up in the sink. To start it all again . . . had she ever even given it a thought? Tom thought perhaps she might have done until she woke up in the morning to the rattle of milk-bottles. Had she then remembered the smell of the moors and the rattle of scree on the Cairngorm tops, the rushing of the icy stream down the glen by Fred and Betty's lawn? Would she go back there, sick with London rooms and the infidelities of men who only wanted her to do the cooking and the washing-up and have a baby to assuage male conceit? No wonder Smiler the dog was the chosen companion, content only to give and love, asking nothing in return. Tom felt deeply guilty and contrite. He had chosen her for his own needs, and fallen in love by default. Now it was catching up with him and he deserved all he got.

He got up and washed and dressed and made coffee. Rod took his in bed, with much groaning.

Tom walked to work. It took ages, and his mind worked overtime all the way, getting nowhere. It was Friday, and he decided to go to Scotland for the weekend. He couldn't face going home to garden and mend the gate. There was absolutely no point in home any more. The self-pity would have got him again if he hadn't got Scotland to think about. He supposed he wanted to go because he thought Camilla might be there. When he got to the office he called his own bluff by ringing Betty.

'Thought I might drive up this weekend. Have you got a spare bed?'

'There's always a spare bed for you, dear. It'll be lovely to see you. Have you found Camilla yet?'

She wasn't there. He scratched a deep mark on the top of his desk with a razor blade that lay handy.

'No.'

'Jo came over last weekend. She's really loving it in Edinburgh.'

Bully for Jo.

Perhaps Betty thought she had been less than tactful, for she added, 'Work is all she thinks of. It takes her mind off things, I suppose.'

'She's always been like that.'

'Oh. Oh well.'

'Good for the nation. Tough on husband. I don't know what time I'll arrive, Betty. I'll ring you again.'

'We're always here, you know that.'

She sounded motherly and sweet and Tom could see her do-gooding eyes gleaming with sympathy behind her thick spectacles. It made him feel good and lucky, although he knew he wasn't. Females like Betty made up for the Ann Forresters of the world. He worked very hard all day. Terry was on holiday, which was restful, but Tom could have used his grumbling and his blue jokes and his throwaway amazing sidelights on his own Casanova progress. Tom's work was going better through neglect than when he had worried about that and nothing else. Life was unjust. Lovely jobs were queueing to jump into his in-tray. The summer lull was over and everyone was fresh and eager to make more money before the Christmas ten-day hibernation. All the same, he was going to Scotland.

He went home to collect his things, slept until four, and took off in the grey light of the distant dawn. Driving really fast on not too busy roads was good for the soul. The sun came up mistily to one of the still, sunny, silent autumn days that Tom loved and the gentle hills of Yorkshire came towards him from the horizon. Although in the car, he could feel the wiry heather underfoot and hear the bumbling bees rooting through the purple flowers. Sour, sour London bedsits and beery Earl's Court, so close in the brain . . . the hills came forward to annul the fumes and stains of city living. Golden fields reached for his silly Porsche and the speed dropped. He opened the windows and heard the river dropping down over the stones, following the road up the valley. His old route . . . habit took him, and he realised that he was hungry, and pulled up by the stone bridge that took the lane up the side valley to the pub. The pub wouldn't be open, but there was a shop with a tea-room beside the post office, and a sort of butcher that sold sausage rolls, he remembered that.

He cut the engine.

Nothing was changed. Why should it be? The cows were already out in the water meadows. There was a 'No Vacancies' sign on the B and B board — it was Saturday and Mrs Haythorn had her regulars for the weekend. Tom got out, feeling cramped and rumpled and city-stained, and wanting a cup of tea. He took some deep breaths, thought he might ring Betty while he was about it.

He went to the phone box and dialed the number. The sale board was down from the abandoned cottage that he had once dreamed of installing Camilla in, he noticed, and the ubiquitous Bed and Breakfast sign was hanging in its place. A wreath of smoke curled from the chimney. I could have bought it, Tom thought, even without Camilla . . . have a flat in town. If he sold the house, and he'd have to soon . . . even if he shared

the proceeds with Jo there'd still be enough.
God, he'd have to tidy his life up shortly. He
was drifting, awash with self-pity. A weekend
with Fred and Betty would spur him to
action.

'Tom! Where are you?'

He told her. 'It won't take me long.'

'There's a slight complication,' Betty said,
hesitant.

'What's that?'

'Jo's coming too. She rang last night. I told
her we were expecting you.'

'What did she say?'

'She said, so what?'

Tom considered, a trifle hurt. Had he made
so very little impact, that she could remember
him without any emotion at all?

'Yeah, well, same here. So what?'

'I knew you'd be civilised about it.'

He could picture Betty beaming with being
proved right.

'We'll see you soon then?'

'Fine.'

He rang off.

He felt nettled. So what? If only he could
have admitted it earlier, it had been so what?
for years. Nothing to look forward to, without
a child. Without Camilla. So what? He went
out of the phone box. He bought a cup of tea
in the tea-room and drank it quickly, without

enjoyment, and got back into the Porsche. So bloody what? Bloody women, bloody life. He had been what he thought of as easy-going, and now saw as negative. His lonely upbringing had made him self-reliant — he thought. But now he realised that he was not. Yet Jo was 'really loving it in Edinburgh', according to Betty's former report — Jo the gregarious, Jo who hated being on her own, Jo who had never been away from her home ground in her life before. Tom felt quite viciously towards her as he drove, having the effrontery to be happy without him, but then he could not help seeing the funny side of this, even in his present state of depression. It was altogether too civilised to think that life wasn't just a muddle of getting by, hoping the decisions one made were the right ones, and making the best of what befell. Jo, with her outgoing, optimistic nature, would make the best of any circumstances, unlike Camilla, the congenital pessimist. This last thought flooded Tom with a fresh, desperate desire for Camilla, so that he knew that all he was suffering from in essence was the age-old agony of lost love. God damn her, didn't she have the sense to come back to him! What was she playing at, stealing bloody dogs for companionship? Did she think even a dog was better than himself?

Tom arrived at Fred and Betty's in the afternoon, wishing he had never set out. Jo being there had changed the visit's function entirely. He actually felt nervous at meeting her again. He sat in the car, prevaricating, waiting outside the headmistress's study. Her car was parked neatly on the drive beside the Landrover. One of the Labradors lay in front of it in the autumn sunshine and the other was scratching itself in the porch. The sound of the motor-mower broke the still, deep silence of the windless day, working behind the house. Tom opened the car door but went on sitting, coming slowly but hopefully to the conclusion that the place was empty of all but Fred, mowing. A lovely afternoon . . . Jo and Betty would have taken the children out along the glen, perhaps with a picnic. There was no headmistress behind the study door.

'Great.' Tom got out and stretched, calmed.

Fred came round the side of the house on the mower and stopped the engine at the sight of Tom's Porsche.

'Hey! You've made good time!'

'The girls out?'

'They've gone to the school fête. Left the dogs with me. They won't be back till sixish. Want a beer?'

'That's great. Thanks. It's good to see you.'

Tom's tension was released. So what, as Jo

so rightly said. The beer helped. They lay in deck-chairs and Tom told Fred about his adventures at the Battersea Dogs Home and said, 'I'm a fool, don't tell me,' and Fred said, 'Well, at least she's alive. She'll turn up.'

'She's not volunteered so far. She doesn't know Jo and I have parted — probably wouldn't put in an appearance if she did know, the way I treated her.'

'It takes time for the dust to settle.'

It seemed an eternity to Tom already, but he didn't argue. He suspected that the subject could well be a bore to Fred, whose love-life appeared to be of minor importance beside the demands of estate maintenance.

'We've got the last bedroom sorted out at last. You could try it tonight, if you like — although it still smells a bit of wax-seal.'

'I can always sleep out if you get punters, you know. I've got my sleeping-bag in the boot. You must get more tourists at weekends?'

'Friends get shoved in with the children if we're busy. It always works out, don't worry. We like friends coming.'

He glanced at his watch.

'They'll be back soon.'

Tom felt his nerves contract at these words, and took a long swig of his beer. The sun had dipped behind the mountains and it was suddenly sharp and damp. Unfriendly.

'The days are drawing in,' Fred said regretfully.

They got up and went indoors.

But it was Jo, when they met again, who was the most emotionally thrown. She had not expected to be. She came home from the fête with a basket full of homemade jam, cake, bread and six raffia place-mats and saw Tom standing in front of the newly-lit fire in the residents' lounge and felt an incredible surge of homesickness seize her: a manic flowering of old memories of loving Tom, that she had to fight to stop herself betraying. The sight of him, so dear, so familiar, shocked her into facing what she had given up. Was she mad? Her first reactions, unexpected, left her dithering before him, holding back from throwing her arms round him. But he smiled and leaned forward and kissed her in his thoroughly civilised, habitual manner, and she managed to pull herself into a semblance of offhand normality, talking about the fête.

Neither of them were anxious to be left alone together and Fred, getting the message, brought drinks into the lounge and Jo slipped away to help Betty get the dinner.

'God, what an idiot I am!' Jo chopped onions, as directed, furiously, and did not

300

know whether the tears were for Tom or the vegetables.

'He's so nice, to leave,' Betty said equably.

'I thought seeing him wouldn't worry me at all!'

'Are you saying it does?'

'Yes!'

'Four will be plenty, and two cloves of garlic. Here. And the parsley needs chopping. Have a baby, why not?'

'Oh, God!'

The chopping knife scored the board viciously.

Jo did not dare say any more. Even Betty! The onion tears poured down her cheeks. She had been so sure, so secure, the past bundled up, tightly secured and thrown away behind her. In six weeks she had built a new life. She had filled every minute of it with hard, mind-blotting work and had felt justified, proud, exhausted, fulfilled. She had not stopped for one moment to think about Tom or Grott or her old home. It was the only way she had seen how to deal with her loss — and whether the loss of her school was greater than the loss of Tom she had never decided. Not until now. But the break with Tom was quite final; she had always known that. So why the helpless, swooning sense of loss at seeing him again, when it was all so cut and

301

dried in her mind?

'I'm stupid, really, to have thought — seeing Tom again wouldn't affect me.'

With hindsight, incredibly insensitive. It was her nature to put her mind away from something she knew she couldn't have; it was part of her success, to build on what was possible. She hadn't bargained for ties of the heart, old Mother Nature and suchlike, biological weaknesses . . . Tom had been such an undemanding man, save about the succession.

'Look, take a drink, and go and talk to him. It's all done here. I'll put this in the oven and see the children into bed, and then we can all have a good talk over dinner. Weeping in the kitchen will get you nowhere.'

'It's the onions.'

But she knew it wasn't.

She did as she was told.

When she came back into the sitting-room, Tom saw her afresh with a sense of great regret, but no more. Her natural vitality and glowing presence was a sham, to his mind. The weight she had lost over her tragedy had improved her figure and she had lost none of her colour and vibrancy; she could find another man if she chose within a week of wanting, to his mind. But he suspected she preferred to stay alone.

'So, what's this new life you're into? You look well on it. I bet it's bloody hard work.'

'I'm teaching mentally-handicapped children. It's wonderful. I love it. And only teaching, no administration — no caretakers to fight with, faulty plumbing to sort out, accounts to keep track of, all that rubbish. Just the children, and their parents, who are quite different from the Tranters of this world. There's no rat-race for their children — just to recognise one letter of the alphabet, or even make one step, is success. It's glorious. So rewarding, so sad, all mixed-up together, and funny as well. It's wonderful.'

'Where is this?' She hadn't written, after all. He had only heard through Betty.

'It's just a small centre, in the Edinburgh suburbs. I've got a flat almost in the city, tiny — it's in the street going up to the castle. I love it, two rooms, that's all. It all needs redecorating, so that takes time, and new curtains — I'm making those. And I go to evening classes — one for painting and one for yoga. It's great living in a city after the country — there's so much going on, concerts and exhibitions all to hand, not a mile's journey there and back. It's hard to fit it all in.'

Tom felt gloomy, not having anything to say in return save that his life carried on in the same boring fashion as it had for the last ten years, only even more boring now he had no wife to talk to. Much as he wanted Jo to be happy in her new life, it was galling to be told just how happy she was without him. He quite saw that getting back to teaching, without all the hassle of administration, would be a great relief but, if he knew his Jo, it would not be long before she would be wanting to boss someone around, tell them how the set-up could be improved. Within five years he had no doubt she would be running the place, or even the whole of the Social Services in Scotland. Her energetic nature had not flagged, merely faltered briefly in the face of adversity.

It was awful having nothing to counter with. He took too much to drink and over supper started to think about Camilla, Camilla in the bed that stood directly above his head, swooning with love and joy at the offer of being a mother to his child — what an idiot he was with his romantic notions of love and happiness and bloody women! His life was an arid road compared to Jo's warehouse of goodies. What was wrong with him? The happy, smiling faces round the table, flushed with good food and wine, all spoke of perfect happiness and fulfilment. And he had lost the lot. He filled her glass.

'Cheer up, Tom,' Betty said.

'He needs Camilla,' Jo said. 'What's happened to Camilla?'

'Camilla's disappeared.'

Drink had dissolved the barriers of reserve, and now that Jo had mentioned Camilla, the subject was thrown open to general discussion. Tom was persuaded to tell Jo about the Battersea Dogs Home episode, which he now found extremely embarrassing.

'Where would she have gone? With a dog. You have to try and think how her mind worked. You know her best.' Jo was nothing if not supportive. 'You must be able to work it out.'

'Not if she wanted to start a new life somewhere. How could you begin to guess?'

'Where did she like? Up here?'

'Not particularly. It's her home, and she didn't like her home. We stayed in Yorkshire, the only time we were together. She liked Yorkshire. There was a cottage — '

He found it impossible to describe their wild and romantic ambitions for that cottage with Jo's eyes upon him. He refilled his wine glass.

Betty took him up eagerly.

'The one for sale? You told me about it. Have you called there since?'

'No. I've passed it. It's occupied again, got

a B and B notice outside. But I rang Mrs Haythorn, and she said Camilla had never been back — I did think about that cottage. It was for let as well as for sale. Camilla has no money — not that I know of — so I knew she couldn't buy it, but it struck me she might possibly manage a lease.'

'She's doing Bed and Breakfast!' Betty's eyes gleamed.

'Camilla?' He couldn't see it. 'I rang you from there this morning. The phone box is at the bottom of the drive.'

'You never looked? You never called?'

'I never thought of it.'

'You're mad!'

'How could she survive there, without a car? A job?'

'Oh, Tom, you've no imagination! She sold her grandmother's old tiara . . . she takes the bus to — where? Where's it near? — '

'Nowhere.'

' . . . The bus to the nearest town then, and works as a secretary. She's a secretary, isn't she?'

'Yes.'

'They're crying out for them in Wharfedale,' Fred said doubtfully.

'She works in the hotel! There's a hotel there. They've given her a job. You give us a better idea then!'

'Jesus, it's not possible!'

Betty had got Tom all worked up. He tried to remember exactly what Mrs Haythorn had said on the phone, that had made him dismiss the idea so entirely. She had said a man had bought the cottage, as far as he could remember. But house sales were notoriously falling through, and he had made his phone call some time ago. Perhaps Camilla had managed to get a lease on it.

'Don't give him ideas, Betty,' Fred reprimanded. 'I should think it's only remotely likely. If she's no money she's got to have a decent job to rent a cottage.'

'But she's doing Bed and Breakfast! We live on Bed and Breakfast, don't we?'

'Well, I suppose . . . it might be worth calling . . .'

Tom wondered whether he had become very drunk or whether Betty's suppositions were causing the pulses to hammer uncomfortably in his brain. What if she had been there all the time . . . this morning, when he phoned . . . talking to Smiler in the kitchen . . . It was as wild a hope as the Battersea Dogs Home, yet that had yielded the most comforting clue of all, that she had not committed suicide.

'She might turn up here some time,' Jo suggested. 'If you were happy here. One day

307

she might come back.'

'You could get a private detective to find her,' Fred said.

'Or the Salvation Army.'

'They don't do lovers' tiffs, surely? Only erring offspring, and ancient brothers and sisters?'

'An advert in *The Times*.'

'She never read *The Times*.'

'The *Guardian* then.'

'A solicitor . . . will hear something to her advantage. That might find her.'

'Am I to her advantage?'

'She used to think so, surely?'

When they went to bed, Tom lay sleepless, aching for Camilla. In this house, it was Camilla who was powerful in the brain, not Jo, although he had stayed longer here with Jo. It was cleared up with Jo now: she did not need him, had never needed him, but they could in the future be good friends in the time-honoured style, quite sincerely, without barbs. Perhaps that was what they had always been, in truth. No more. He lay staring at Fred's newly-painted ceiling, where all the cracks had been covered over, and watched the autumn half-moon sailing over the hilltop above the glen, framed between the newly-waxed window-sashes. He felt strung up, taut, on the edge of an abyss between past and future. Something had to happen. He could not drift on.

★   ★   ★

Jo too lay awake after supper, reflecting on her relationship with Tom, not unhappily. She did not believe in being unhappy. It was a relief to have got this meeting over, with its unexpected emotions. She felt that the marriage pact was now signed off, concluded without pain, although she knew she loved Tom and would always love Tom. Perhaps her independent nature would never require a man in the way that hopeless Camilla seemed to require support. She could accept loneliness; it was part of the price one paid for the ultimate freedom.

And even now, the emotional events so recently surmounted, her mind was burrowing ahead, anticipating her return to Edinburgh to her little eyrie high in the grey cliff-face of the Edinburgh tenement. Unwittingly she had given her rooms the same character as her office at her old school: her own personality could have full rein, unchecked by Tom's austere taste. Her mind, now untrammelled by the chores of headmistresshood, was free to roam on colour-schemes and curtain lengths and basket-chairs. The creaking sash could be raised to the muted, friendly noise of confused traffic below, to the hulloaing of trains coming into Waverly Station, the hubbub of a tourist pack advancing towards the castle. It was all new and fresh to her tired, country-softened brain. She loved the feeling of being in the middle of a beautiful city, and the joy of nipping down straight into streets full of interest and excitement and historical ambience, utterly refreshing after the arid functionalism of her old new town, a city off-the-peg, ready-to-wear, abysmally failing in style. She had not known what she was missing. And her funny, darling, hopeless, hideous children waiting for her attention, her affection, which she could give unstintingly, without looking at the clock, without wondering if she could get to the butcher's before it closed or the dry-cleaner's for Tom's suit. Poor Tom! She had swapped him for her own selfish indulgence, to stay barren, to triumph in the ultimate freedom: total independence.

It was marvellous to have had this meeting, to have the opportunity to write Tom off, conclusively. Even still loving him, she wanted him to go. Tomorrow they would drive off in different directions. They would send Christmas cards. There would be no grieving.

★ ★ ★

Smiler, let out for his evening bedtime piddle, trotted down the drive towards the telephone box. Unused to the open spaces and smells of the countryside, he stood and barked at a late passing car. He lamented the absence of the heady trails of menstruating London bitches, but he knew a good berth when he met one, and when his peculiar new owner called him in out of the darkness, he complied without hesitation, head down for the kitchen door.

## THE END

We do hope that you have enjoyed reading this large print book.

Did you know that all of our titles are available for purchase?

We publish a wide range of high quality large print books including:
**Romances, Mysteries, Classics**
**General Fiction**
**Non Fiction and Westerns**

Special interest titles available in large print are:
**The Little Oxford Dictionary**
**Music Book**
**Song Book**
**Hymn Book**
**Service Book**

Also available from us courtesy of Oxford University Press:
**Young Readers' Dictionary**
**(large print edition)**
**Young Readers' Thesaurus**
**(large print edition)**

For further information or a free brochure, please contact us at:
**Ulverscroft Large Print Books Ltd.,**
**The Green, Bradgate Road, Anstey,**
**Leicester, LE7 7FU, England.**
**Tel:** (00 44) 0116 236 4325
**Fax:** (00 44) 0116 234 0205

## SOUTH LANARKSHIRE LIBRARIES

## HOUSEBOUND  SERVICE

| | | | |
|---|---|---|---|
| 1075 | 94 | 81 | 1089 |
| 411 | 143 | | 4098 |
| 1055 | 378 | | 2047 |
| 733 | | | 4048 |
| 1118 | | | 2009 |
| 645 | | | |
| 130 | | | |
| 34 | | | |
| )29 | | | |